A
Night
Claimed

by

DOMINA
ALEXANDRA

2019

A Night Claimed © 2019 Domina Alexandra
Triplicity Publishing, LLC

ISBN-13: 978-1-970042-01-6
ISBN-10: 1-970042-01-X

Printed in the United States of America
First Edition – 2019
Cover Design: Triplicity Publishing, LLC
Editor: Ashley Hutchison - Triplicity Publishing, LLC

I have to thank my editor at Triplicity, Ashley Hutchison. I know Bonnie had a lot of personality to tame. To my Beta reader, fellow author, and friend, Lynn Lawler. I'd like to thank Tessa Moore for introducing me to Mill City. It's officially on the map. To Hannbrain for playing word twister with me until my title was born, and Ninja for seeing my book come to life through your own eyes. Finally, Bonnie gives a shout out to the Fantasy World believers. What she knew to be fiction, came true for her. So, you fantasy fans, don't stop believing. Imagination was created for a reason.

This book is for all the medical professionals who work endless beside me!

Chapter One

The red and blue lights temporarily blinded me as I darted around the ambulance. It was windy tonight, causing strands of my hair to blow across my face. Looking back toward the front of the ambulance, I suddenly understood how people felt who encountered the incredible brightness of the lights on the roads. The sirens were off. I pulled out the Lifepak cardiac monitor and airway bag from the back of the rig and then rushed to the entrance of the bar. I wasn't entirely sure of the time, but I knew it was after midnight. My partner and I had been picking up drunks left and right all night, which was fairly standard for a Friday.

The acrid smell of cigarettes overpowered my senses once I stepped through the front door of the bar. I winced noticeably for a moment, but I managed to regain my composure. The interior was reminiscent of an early 1990s sitcom bar, wherein regulars jealously guarded their preferred spots. Several pool tables were situated in neat rows to the right. Noisy slot machines were placed against the wall near the tables, luring gamblers with neon colors and carnivalesque sales pitches. Country music blared through the speakers on the jukebox. Round tables occupied the side left of the bar counter in the center. A thick haze of cigarette smoke settled over the tables where a few people were playing cards. *I thought smoking was no longer allowed in public places. Maybe I'm wrong?*

My partner, Jr., took the airway bag from me and set about trying to find our patient. He nodded to the fire crew who had arrived earlier and were already preparing to assist. A few of the crew lingered close to the patient, trying to convince him to leave with us in the ambulance so that we could treat him properly. I gently put the equipment on the floor, careful not to cause alarm by an abrupt sound, and then cautiously approached him. I was glad I succeeded in avoiding the goopy pile of vomit next to him. The smell was rancid, but it wasn't a smell with which I was unfamiliar, and I was determined to ignore it.

"Let me talk to him."

"We got this," came the response from a member of the fire crew. It was a clear attempt to dismiss me.

He appeared to be fresh out of the academy. I narrowed my eyes at him before taking the opportunity to get a look at the others who were with him. All men. Even the captain was a man. Not uncommon. His thick mustache concealed his upper lip completely, and when he smiled at me in acknowledgement of my presence, I felt uncomfortable. It was clearly a forced smile. It seemed that the only person here who would respect me, and my position, was Jr.

He stepped around the clustered fire crew to better inspect the patient. He looked to me. "How do you want to approach?"

It was infuriating to be forced to constantly remind male coworkers that a woman could handle a drunk man as well as the next person. Probably better, particularly in my case. My father was a chronic drunk. At least, that's what my family always called him. Being labeled an alcoholic was something my father refused to tolerate. It was impossible for me to hate him however, not simply because he was my father, but because of the way he captured everyone's affections with the warmth of his spirit. Despite my father's demons, he was still my light.

I ignored them, focusing instead on the patient. His long, dark hair was matted as if he hadn't combed it in days. His skin was flushed, and the biting odor of liquor seeped from his pores.

"I'm sure you don't like all this attention on you – all of these men standing around you in blue uniforms."

The man sat slouched on the floor, wedged between two barstools. His legs were outstretched. He didn't respond. His head hung low against his chest. I watched his shoulders rise and fall, and I knew then he must be laboring hard to breathe normally in his odd position on the floor. I grabbed the stool to his right to make enough space to work, sliding it out of the way slowly to keep him calm.

I locked eyes with the youngest man on the fire crew and asked, "Can you move the other stool out of the way?" I returned my attention to the patient on the floor. "We're not cops. Only paramedics."

"I'm dizzzzy." It was hard to hear him since his head was barely raised and he was slurring his words.

"I'm sure you are." I knelt in front of him and retrieved a BioHoop bag from my back pocket meant for the collection of vomit and offered it to him. "In case you feel like you're going to throw up."

Without hesitating, he pressed his face into the opening of the bag. A lumpy, beige liquid emerged from between his lips. The BioHoop caught most of it, but the rest spilled out onto my gloved hands in gloppy rivulets. I felt an intense urge to jerk my hands away, but I forced them to remain in place. He continued for a few minutes more and then his belly was still. I hastily removed my gloves once he was finished. The squelching sound they made while being stuffed into the bag nearly cost me the contents of my own stomach. I gulped with some difficulty, remembering that maintaining a collected demeanor was paramount, then reached into my side pocket for a new pair.

"Feeling any better?" I asked.

"No," he groaned. He attempted to rid himself of the taste of his vomit by spitting. He lacked both the strength and coordination to keep his saliva from oozing down his chin and then his shirt.

"My name's Bonnie. I think it's best we take you to the hospital. You might have alcohol poisoning."

He shook his head with some effort. "Not my first rodeo, miss."

"I don't doubt that." I smiled. "In fact, you might recognize me. I've picked you up before. Twice, actually."

Hearing that made him eager to get a good look at me. He sluggishly lifted his head. His pupils were dilated. He was disoriented. He squinted, searching my face for some feature that would jog his memory through the haze of smoke in the bar.

After a few seconds he said, "Oh, yeah."

"I am pretty sure you told me that I was the best paramedic you ever had." *Okay, that may be a bit of an exaggeration, but oh, well. I'm certain he commented on my looks, though. Quite inappropriately.*

He nodded groggily. "Yeah. You were. And cute."

4

He tried to smile charmingly, but he failed spectacularly, looking instead like one of those predators you see in a mug shot with a missing front tooth.

"So how about we make it three for three?" I was not going to entertain his unwelcome compliment. I'd spent much of my career dealing with men who assumed I was simply a pretty face.

The man made no reply.

I tilted my head in the direction of the gurney behind me. "Let's get you on the gurney. I'll start an I.V. and get some fluids into your body. A little Zofran for the dizziness and nausea. How does that sound?"

"You'll be in the back with me?" he asked nervously, glancing at the all-male fire crew.

"You bet." I put my hand on his shoulder and squeezed. "They're not cops, I assure you. Just here to help like me."

He exhaled shakily through his lips. "Okay."

"That's what I love to hear." I rose from my knees and turned to face Jr., but I kept my fingertips on the patient's shoulder. "Let's put another blanket on top of the gurney."

Jr. grinned and he reached behind the gurney to grab an extra blanket. "Glad you're coming with us, sir. I'm Jr. Do you remember me?"

From his position on the floor the patient examined Jr. with the skepticism of a conspiracy theorist. He shook his head emphatically.

"Of course not, he only remembers the pretty ones," joked the youngest of the fire crew.

Keeping quiet when he spoke was proving to be a difficult task. I inhaled deeply and regained my focus. I'd have to have a conversation with this fledgling later about professionalism and his not-so-vague sexist remarks.

As soon as we got the patient on the gurney and strapped him to it, I waved to the entire fire crew. "We got it from here."

"You don't want one of us to ride in the back?"

"Nope. I'm good."

The captain frowned, his bulky arms crossed over his chest were the only form of silent protest he exhibited at that moment. "I insist."

I didn't visibly react. "The patient is well-behaved. You guys can go on. Have a good night."

I didn't wait for his response. They wanted to provoke me, and I was in no mood to give into their sexist carping.

*

I leaned over the counter at the nurse's station, chatting absentmindedly with the charge nurse once we had ensured the man who we picked up at the bar was registered and cooperating with the hospital staff.

"How about you guys take a break and stop bringing us drunks and overdoses?" The charge nurse tittered playfully as she shuffled and organized small stacks of paper.

I shrugged. "Trust me, we don't go out searching for them."

I gave her some nondescript farewell after that and turned around to find myself nearly face-to-face with Nurse Summers. She was putting on a fresh pair of gloves. The clipboard under her left arm wobbled a bit as she pulled the gloves over each wrist hurriedly. She braced her arm against her side, trying to keep the clipboard from falling to the ground before she finished. Her full name was Rosemary Summers, and she was the best RN working in this hospital. She was also very beautiful and very heterosexual. Her pear-green eyes were so striking that it was easy to forget yourself when you encountered them, and they were the perfect complement to her auburn hair. Rosemary was indeed a heartbreaker. Jr. was undeniably enchanted by her.

The abrasive squeak of shoes against the linoleum floors found me in mid-reverie. The sight of hospital security roughly escorting a man out of the building forcefully shoved my consciousness back into my body. I recognized him immediately as one of the hospital's frequent flyers. He would call 911 for anything. If he stubbed his toe, he'd be in the emergency room. He spent more time coming to this hospital in the last several years than the staff. I even brought him in myself a time or two.

He must have sensed my eyes on him. His head twisted toward me and my spine stiffened. He screeched in an unsettling pitch and then launched at the closest target: Nurse Summers. His hands appeared from behind his back like dark talons, escaping the vice-like grip of the security officers. They sliced through the air, grasping for Summers. She was eerily calm and motionless. Before he could reach her however, the security team snatched his hands from the air and pinned them him behind his back. He was frantically struggling against the officers as they pushed his body down on the floor. Summers was still, seemingly transfixed by him. I couldn't understand this steadiness of hers in this choppy experience.

"You okay?" I cautiously touched her arm, noticing her clenched fist. Summers's skin was hotter than hellfire. I jerked my arm away. "Rosemary!"

She blinked a few times at the sound of her name and her body began to relax a little. Even at a moment like this she was exquisite.

Summers shook her head and rubbed her eyes. She didn't look at me. "He caught me off guard. Thank you."

I wasn't quite sure what she was thanking me for, but I went along with it. I pursed my lips in an attempt to keep myself from saying anything about her strange demeanor during the attack. "I'll make sure to take him to another hospital if he's ever again in our rig."

Summers rattled her arms like tree limbs in a windstorm and a grunt of disgust erupted from her mouth. "I want to go for a run." Her phone rang. "I'll see you later. I hope the rest of your shift is better."

She was gone.

"You see that?" Jr. asked as he gesticulated wildly.

"See what?"

"Summers! She looked like she was going to kick that guy's ass!" Jr. clapped his hands animatedly, his eyes wide with either horror or surprise. Maybe both. I wasn't sure.

I rolled my eyes. I knew that he would spend the next hour gushing about Summers like a teenager experiencing his first crush. I sucked in a deep breath through my teeth and prepared myself for the inane conversation to come as we headed to the rig. I fell asleep listening to Jr.'s nauseating monologue in the passenger seat.

*

The shrill chime of my alarm ripped me from the womblike feeling of deep slumber. I grumbled frustratedly. Even though I kept crazy hours at work I never liked sleeping in late. Today, it was a bit more difficult to get myself moving for some reason. Still lying on my stomach, I reached for my phone, opening one eye so I could see to turn off the alarm. The irritating chime was finally silent, and I sighed in relief. It was the afternoon.

I can't believe I slept this late.

At least there was enough time left in the day to go out. I checked my phone for messages while rolling onto my back. I had a few texts from one of my friends who lived in Mill City here in Oregon. I'd been neglecting him for a while. I promised him a couple of days ago that I would visit tonight. I texted back, assuring him I was indeed coming, then let my body go limp for a several minutes as I attempted to persuade myself to get out of bed. Minutes quickly became a few hours because I decided to catch up on some reading.

Now hungry, I had no choice but to leave my bedroom. A hot shower beforehand would probably be the best way to coax myself fully awake. I studied my image in the mirror afterwards. Everyone constantly compared me to Nicole Beharie from the hit television series, *Sleepy Hollow*. I did not mind the comparison, though there were differences between us two: my skin was a bit lighter than hers, somewhere between caramel and honey. Also, when I smiled, deep dimples formed on either side of my mouth.

"Time to go out," I instructed my reflection.

A Night Claimed

I left without seeing my roommates. *They must be out.* The last orange rays of sunlight burst through the purple clouds in riotous dissent. It was still early in the evening, but by the time I grabbed some food and made it to Highway 22, it looked as though a black blanket had been flung across the sky.

The stretch of Highway 22 right outside of Mill City was bereft of street lights. I was on edge, snapping my gaze left, right, then forward over and over again. I hated driving at night. *Maybe a little music might help me calm down.* Although I was familiar with the positions of the radio buttons, I found myself fumbling around for a few moments while trying to keep my eyes on the road. But before my fingertips found any buttons, I saw red, flashing lights 40 yards ahead. They were hazard lights.

The swirling battle in my mind between my paramedic and civilian instincts had physical manifestations: beads of perspiration formed at each of my temples, and I started shivering with the competing worries. My car's speed decreased, and I realized then which instinct had prevailed. News reports and local gossip of situations exactly like this never ended well. The urge to retch seized my throat, but I refused to yield. I swallowed forcibly and put the car in park. I was intensely aware of the quiet. No chirping crickets, no yowling coyotes, not even a rustling of wild rabbits. Only the *click-click-click* of the hazard lights from the stationary car in front of mine.

Reason wriggled its way through the unease, and I retrieved my phone from the cup holder in the center console and snapped a quick photo of my surroundings. I also made sure to share my location with my friend in Mill City, just in case. I opened my door and tentatively

10

stepped out of the car. My eyes zipped around as I walked to the trunk, and it was only when I was pulling the latch to open it that I realized I hadn't yet checked to see if there was anyone in the other vehicle. *Damn it!* I almost shut the trunk but decided against it. There were things I needed to grab first: flares, flashlight, medical kit, knife, and my laminated EMS jacket. I slid the knife into my pocket, slipped into the jacket, and then arranged the other items under my left arm so I could carry the flashlight in my right hand. I flicked the switch and the bulb of the flashlight flickered and then emanated a steady stream of light.

"Hello?" I called as I approached the car.

Nothing. No sound at all.

Maybe this person was crazy enough to go walking down the road? Not the smartest idea, but possible. I called out a few more times, a little louder than before, but silence was the only answer I received. *Well, I tried.* I turned on my heel and started back toward my car.

"Help." The plea was barely audible. I spun to face the abandoned car again. "I fell. Please…"

Muffled sobbing followed the plea.

I couldn't find the source of the voice. It seemed as if it was all around me. I shook my head. *Impossible.* I tucked the flashlight under my chin and reached into my pocket for my phone. I dialed 911.

WHAM!

Everything I had been carrying fell out of my arms as I was propelled forward. I twisted my body sideways to minimize the impact. I met the ground with terrible force and a wave of pain rippled through my right hip, my ribs, and then finally, my head. I moaned aloud, quickly reaching up to my head to make sure I wasn't bleeding. Thankfully, I hadn't been knocked unconscious, but I couldn't move without considerable effort. *I don't think anything is broken. Fuck. Thank God. What the hell happened?* I strained my head and body to try to get a look at what had hit me.

Bristly, thick fur brushed against the nape of my neck.

A scream echoed off the trees. It was mine.

I scrambled into a crouched position, momentarily forgetting the pain pulsing throughout my muscles. There was nothing. The flashing of red from the clicking hazards of the car for which I'd stopped continued. Burying my fingers into the grass, my breathing quickened. My fingers drew together to create a fist, then released. I inhaled sharply, then allowed my hands to dive deeply into the dry tufts and weeds, searching for my phone, for the flashlight, for my flares, for anything at all. I heard the soft, begging voice once again.

I did not respond this time. I persisted in my search. The familiar, sturdy plastic of my phone's case was at last discovered underneath my fingertips. I gripped the phone tightly and rose from my crouched position. I wobbled. I wobbled again. I kept my grip on the phone and steadied myself. I listened for the voice, for whatever had slammed into me.

Click-click-click.

The air was ominously heavy, and my resolve began to buckle under its weight. There were eyes watching from somewhere in the darkness. There was no doubt about that. Panic spread through my bloodstream like a greedy virus. I sprinted to my car. Quick, ragged breaths were all that I could manage since my concentration was staunchly fixed on my door handle. I barely grazed the steel of my car before my worry for the desperate stranger returned. I set my feet firmly in place, trying to convince myself not to leave when there was clearly someone in distress.

"Can you walk?" I yelled into the darkness.

Nothing. Again.

The crunch of breaking glass was the first thing I heard. I tasted the bitter iron of my own blood. Pain ripped into my flesh like a monster ripping through its prey. But the monster was real. The creature was real. It was on top of me – an enormous, black mass had me pinned on the hood of my car in the time it took to blink once. Struggling to see through my now foggy vision, a form developed with each *click* of the hazards accompanied by the menacing glow of yellow eyes. It was a wolf. A *very big* wolf.

I screamed.

A low growl erupted from its jaws and the ear-splitting screech of its claws scraping against the metal of the car's hood below forced me into a catatonic stillness. A viscous liquid slithered across my face. There was no way to know whether it was blood, tears, or the saliva that was oozing from between the teeth of the wolf. Maybe it was a mixture. I suddenly remembered the knife in my pocket. It was my only option, the only way I had a chance of survival. The black beast kept its yellow eyes on me as I slowly edged my hand along the hood of the car to my pocket, careful not to draw the attention of those nightmarish eyes. I regretted not having the knife in my hand from the start. It was partially exposed, so I was able to grasp it unnoticed. Or so I thought. The wolf peered at me as if it somehow knew what I was trying to do. Its lips tightened in warning. It was a warning I did not heed. I needed to move.

The pain of the wolf's bite was all-consuming. The fragile flesh of my shoulder was no match for the titanium strength of its jaws. Guttural shrieks broke free of my throat, vanishing into the darkness. Vomit bubbled up from my belly and filled my mouth. I coughed violently, spraying jellylike chunks which attached themselves to the wolf's fur. It burrowed its teeth deeper, tearing through tissue and bone.

I reached out with my right hand, feeling around for anything on the hood of the car I could use. The sharp end of broken glass sliced my arm, but I ignored it. I moved my arm up, allowing my hand to close around the oddly-shaped shard of glass that had been expelled from the windshield when my body was thrown against it. It was slightly bigger than my hand. Blood poured from the wounds it was creating in my grip. There was no time to care about that. I quickly sunk the shard into its neck, feeling the wolf's skin and my own split beneath the pressure of the glass.

The monster withdrew and yowled, shaking its head to try to rid itself of the shard still lodged in its neck. This was my chance. I rolled off the hood of the car, falling to the ground. In a weak state, I frantically reached for the handle on the door. I lifted the it quickly, nearly hyperventilating from shock.

A crushing pain exploded in my ribs.

There was nothing after that.

There was only the lingering memory of those yellow eyes.

Chapter Two

"Page Dr. Macgomery."

Through the dreamlike fog I recognized the voice of Rosemary Summers. I opened my eyes slowly, then I remembered the wolf, and my eyes darted around the room, hunting frenziedly for the hellish creature. Summers came to my side and held me down.

"Bonnie, listen to me. Listen! You were attacked by an animal. A man was driving by and saw you being attacked. Luckily, he had a gun." She loosened her grip on my arms. "You won't be able to speak yet because we had to intubate, but you can nod. Do you remember what happened?"

I nodded hesitantly.

"I will take care of you. I promise," she cooed sweetly. The sincerity in her tone made me feel safe.

I was so overwhelmed with relief that I began crying. The doctor entered from the hallway, followed closely by a nurse and a tech. He started talking to me, but I couldn't focus on his words at all. I was alive. Alive. Alive. Alive. Nothing else mattered at that moment. My tears blurred my vision and the doctor's voice faded.

I fell asleep to the sound of Rosemary humming a soothing tune as she worked.

*

A Night Claimed

My skin was hot. Blistering. My mouth felt as if it had been stuffed with cotton. I pressed the call button for a nurse. Something was off. Wrong.

Rosemary came in a short time after. She looked at me and then said, "I'm sorry, but this visit has to be cut short."

"What's wrong with her?"

Jr.! How long has he been here?

"Please, for now, go to the ICU waiting room and I'll find you soon with an update."

There was no argument. I heard the door close and a wave of nausea rushed upwards in my digestive tract. Rosemary held a vomit bag to my lips. Something that looked just like water was expelled with each heave of my stomach, and when I finished, Rosemary disposed of the bag and checked my temperature. She grimaced.

"What is it?" I asked, my voice trembling.

"103.1." She muttered something else afterwards, but I couldn't make it out for the ringing in my ears.

"Why are you here?" I croaked.

"What do you mean?" she asked absentmindedly, pressing a button on the monitor to check my vitals. The blood pressure cuff began to squeeze my arm tightly.

I forgot I had asked her a question. My head hurt from the ringing in my ears, which had now become much louder. I squinted, finding the light in the room suddenly too bright. Rosemary shouted to someone I couldn't see, and relief settled into my chest as the lights dimmed. She replaced my saline bag and dextrose.

"Your sugar keeps dropping. Your body is burning your glucose too quickly."

"Why are you here?" I asked again. Now I was sure I had already asked that question. *Did she answer me?*

"I took a few shifts in ICU so I could take care of you. I wanted to make sure you would be okay."

"Thanks," I replied feebly, shivering uncontrollably against the chill in the hospital air.

"I'm going to see if the doctor can come up with a solution to get your fever down."

I think I nodded. I couldn't be sure. She turned off the lights and exited the room quietly. I slipped into the cool embrace of sleep once again and didn't awaken until I heard Rosemary whispering by the door to my room. I pried my eyes open slightly. I could barely make out the shape of her body, but I was able to determine that she was speaking to someone on a cell phone.

"She's still alive, thank God No, I don't think she knows..." Rosemary turned to me and smiled upon seeing that I was awake. "I have to go. Yes. Yes." She hung up the phone, offering me a sympathetic smile. "How do you feel?"

I was too exhausted to entertain suspicions or ask any more questions.

"Like I was attacked by a very big wolf." My voice was rough, probably from the combination of screaming and having a tube stuck down my throat.

"Seems you are feeling a little better now." Rosemary checked my vitals. "You've been out two days since you were last awake."

My stomach growled, and I thought of the wolf. The yellow eyes.

"You will never face him again," she said in a deep, almost inhuman tone.

Him?

"If you keep improving like this, you'll be out of this hospital within a week," she advised, tapping the screen of the monitor to draw my attention. "How about some food?"

"If it's hospital food, I'm not interested."

Rosemary shook her head. She held up her index finger and disappeared into the hallway, returning a minute later with a brown paper bag in hand. Rosemary reached into the bag and pulled out two big, pulled-pork sandwiches. My eyes widened. The growling in my stomach intensified.

"Jr. brought it. He told me it's your favorite."

She helped me into a sitting position, and I snatched the sandwich from her hand, unwrapping the foil and devouring it in less than two minutes. My gut was churning, and my hands quaked like a drug addict experiencing withdrawal, but I didn't care. Rosemary had the second one already unwrapped for me before I finished the first. I swiped it and inhaled it just as quickly as I ate the first sandwich. I wanted more.

"He's bringing more food in a few hours. Can't hide that much good food in this hospital." She giggled. "Our little secret."

I smiled. "Definitely."

We talked for a while until exhaustion returned for me. Sometime during our conversation, I floated away. It was a much sweeter sleep this time.

Chapter Three

I dressed in the clean clothes Jr. brought from my house. The bandages covering my shoulder were rigid, so I had to dress with caution. The room was silent except for the sound of fabric against skin. I was grateful to Jr. for this silence. He somehow succeeded in keeping my roommates from visiting, which was fine with me. I didn't want to see them. I didn't want to go home.

Last night I was reshaped into something *other*, but I wasn't certain what that something was – as if the cells in my body had shifted. However, the change was imperceptible to the doctor. The tests, the blood panels, the endless poking and prodding. Everything was normal, save for my miraculously swift recovery. But apparently, that could be easily attributed to my youth and good health. I never really expected him to say anything different.

Just outside the door to my room I heard two distinct voices speaking in low, serious tones. I recognized one of the voices as belonging to Rosemary. I peeked around the curtain surrounding my bed which I had drawn in order to change, trying to get a better look at who she was talking to. Through the glass panel of the door I spied a woman facing Rosemary.

Her posture was stiff, the angles of her body were extreme. She looked like the living embodiment of a geometric shape. As she spoke to Rosemary, the coffee-colored hair she had swept up into a ponytail rocked from side to side. Contempt seeped from the pores of her olive skin. My eyes locked with this woman and I was still. For only a second, I noticed her displeasure. I looked down at myself and cursed. I was still without a shirt, and I noted that I had lost some weight.

When I looked up, she was gone, leaving only Rosemary in hallway. I watched as she fidgeted with her chin and then her hair, her gaze lowered. *What was that about?* I slipped into my shirt. I was more concerned with the throbbing in my shoulder for the meantime.

I moved from the curtain as Rosemary entered the room. "You should eat something soon."

"I plan on it." I zipped up my jeans and turned to see Rosemary standing next to a wheelchair. "Really?"

Rosemary shrugged.

"I feel fine." She rolled her eyes in response and so I changed the subject. "Who was that woman you were talking to?"

Rosemary started to reply but stopped herself, then said, "She's an old friend. Why do you ask?"

"I don't know. She just...didn't belong."

Rosemary stiffened. She motioned for me to get into the wheelchair and I did so grudgingly. While wheeling me out of the hospital, she tried to keep the conversation light. I couldn't pay attention, though. My mind was full of yellow eyes and a body with far too many right angles.

*

"You think she really wouldn't like a party?" The voice belonged to Alicia, one of my roommates.

I sat up in the darkness of my bedroom. My legs were comfortably entangled in the cool sheets that embraced my mattress. In spite of this, I couldn't fall asleep, even with the aid of painkillers. I checked the time on my phone. *Eleven.* I blew air between my lips exasperatedly.

"I don't know. She didn't seem interested when I suggested we do something to celebrate her recovery." It was Sandy, my other roommate.

Clearly, they wanted me to get out of bed if they were standing outside of my room talking about me. I had no desire to listen any longer, and I certainly wasn't going to be able to fall asleep. At least, not anytime soon. I untangled my legs from the sheets and hopped out of bed, trying to straighten my pajamas as I moved. I fumbled around in the dark for a minute, looking for my bedroom door. Once I found the doorknob, I opened the door quickly, half-expecting to find my roommates right outside, but the hallway was empty. I heard the television in the living room, so I followed the noise and found both of my roommates sitting on the couch eating pizza.

I frowned.

"Join us," Sandy urged after she spotted me coming into the living room.

I still wasn't tired, but I thought I might be able to drain enough of my energy in order to sleep if I did eat some pizza. I grabbed a slice and started munching away. I fell onto the small sofa, laying my legs over one arm and resting my head against the other end. I could feel the eyes of my roommates boring into me.

"What?"

"You hungry?" Alicia asked sarcastically some time later. "You ate nearly the entire pizza."

I looked over at the pizza box. They were right, but I wasn't baited by the comment. Thankfully, there was another box, and I dug into it with gusto.

When I was done, I surveyed the damage. "I'll pay for the pizzas."

"It's all right," Sandy assured me. "Let us take care of it as a way of welcoming you back home."

"We are happy you have an appetite at all," Alicia added. "And we were thinking that maybe..."

"Alicia!" Sandy snapped, narrowing her eyes at Alicia.

Alicia was undeterred. "How would you feel about having a party? You know, as a way for everyone to welcome you back?"

"For surviving a wolf attack." It was a statement, not a question. I was beginning to feel irritated by their needling. A party wasn't what I wanted right now.

"Well...yeah," Alicia replied carefully, sensing my frustration.

Sandy raised her arms in defeat. "It was only a thought. If you're not up for it, it's absolutely fine."

"Honestly, I don't know." I sighed, fatigue finally beginning to set in. "Right now, I want to go to sleep. But I promise I'll think about it."

I stood up, leaving behind the remains of my one-woman feast, and made my way back to my room. I already knew that I would refuse the party, but I didn't want to be rude, especially when they were only trying to cheer me up.

"Night," Sandy and Alicia called to me as I reached my door.

I didn't respond. I shut the door behind me, flung myself onto my bed, and let sleep take me.

*

I cautiously approached the car, its red hazard lights flashing menacingly as if in warning. But I was too stubborn. A small voice was calling, crying out in the darkness. I had to find the source of the pleas.

Click-click-click-click.

My breathing quickened. It was dark. It was too dark. A low growl echoed in the blackness. I froze. Yellow eyes. Yellow eyes. Yellow eyes.

A hellish and otherworldly scream. It was mine.

I awoke drenched in sweat. *Another nightmare.* I grabbed the bottle of water I left on the nightstand last night and gulped it down in two seconds. The air was heavy with a myriad of smells, some I could identify, others I could not. I tossed the covers aside and got out of bed. *A drive might help.* I tried to change in haste, but I was delayed when I noticed that I could move without pain. I unraveled my bandages and discovered that the massive wound from the wolf bite healed entirely. I was stunned. I needed to investigate. I needed to get out of the house.

*

"You shouldn't be here, Bonnie."

Thanks for the warm welcome, Rosemary.

I knew I shouldn't have come to the hospital. It was just a nightmare. But I honestly didn't know where else I could go in the middle of the night. I did not want to be at home. The sound of the clicking hazards lurked in my eardrums.

"Here." Rosemary handed me a napkin. "It's late. You should be home."

I wiped the sweat from my forehead while I studied Rosemary. She was the only one who brought me any comfort since the incident, and I couldn't pinpoint why. Her features softened as she met my gaze – her cheekbones, her jaw, her lips. They all appeared fuller than they had only moments ago.

"You hungry? We have pizza in the break room." Clearly, Rosemary was going to be the one carrying the weight of this conversation.

I grinned toothily at the question. My appetite suddenly returned. "Absolutely."

I left her in the room and sprinted to the breakroom, my mind only focused on one thing: pizza. *It's not a bad idea, right?* But I never made it there. As soon as I crossed the threshold into the ER, the biting, iron scent of blood suffocated my nostrils. The wound on my shoulder ached, and a hunger like I'd never experienced exploded in my gut. My eyes narrowed in pursuit, searching for the source of the smell.

A stretcher *whooshed* past me surrounded by a bevy of paramedics. A man drenched in blood that was pouring from deep, jagged cuts wailed and struggled against the pain. I felt my consciousness slip away and something else rose to take its place. I lunged forward – a thing, a creature of undiluted impulse, advancing for the most basic of needs. That syrupy, mineral liquid of life. The thrill of flesh tearing apart.

I never caught my prey.

Supernaturally strong arms enveloped me. I shrieked and struggled, but the arms only drew around me more tightly. They spun me, dragged me into the breakroom, and then slammed me against the wall. They were Rosemary's. Before I could react, she locked the door and turned to face me. Her face was no longer soft, no longer full. Rosemary's cheekbones were sharp edges, her jaws were straight lines.

"Bonnie," she snarled. "Bonnie, calm down!"

I blinked rapidly, my chest caving in with each breath I expelled. Confused, I looked to Rosemary hoping for an explanation. She pulled me into a hug, and I relaxed in her embrace.

"Only a panic attack. We are fine," Rosemary purred, stroking the middle of my back. "Focus on your breathing. I'm right here."

I only nodded.

"Stay here." She squeezed my hand and left the room.

She didn't need to say anything. There was no way I was going to make an appearance after that display.

While I waited for her to return, I wondered if I had actually suffered a panic attack or mental break. It was possible, given what I had endured, but it didn't feel like it was anything so commonplace as either of those options. The longer I puzzled over the possibilities, the more I realized that this would not be explained so easily.

"Well, I'm dipping out early. We are going to take a trip." Rosemary smiled reassuringly when she reentered the room.

"With you? Where?" I wasn't in the mood for a trip anywhere except home.

"You trust me?" Rosemary asked.

25

A Night Claimed

It didn't really sound like a question. It was a challenge.

Chapter Four

"Turn right after the gas station," Rosemary instructed.

I did as she directed and followed the road until we arrived in downtown Mill City.

It was tiny, a bit smaller than a football stadium. That did not bother me. In fact, it was a welcome sight at this moment. The drive here had taken us across a long stretch of Highway 22, and to say it nearly destroyed my ability to maintain self-control would be quite an understatement. If Rosemary sensed my discomfort, she made no mention of it while we rode together. Her eyes were ever forward, keeping track of our movements.

We had to cross a bridge to exit downtown. It was further ahead, past a few clusters of houses and several patches of land overcrowded with brambles and ivy. It was quiet, but this type of quiet was peaceful, not ominous. I was starting to settle into my seat, finally feeling a bit relaxed with the distance between us and Highway 22, when Rosemary pointed to a driveway on the left side of the road. I pulled off the road and put the car in park in front of a large, iron gate that blocked the driveway. There was a camera covered in moss at the top of the gate. Surprisingly, it appeared to be functional.

Rosemary stepped out of the car and marched over to the gate, stopping inches away from the iron bars of its doors. I hadn't yet questioned her motives, but I was beginning to wonder why we were in such a remote area. It was a bit unnerving. I tried to ignore the gnawing in my belly. It was impossible to believe that Rosemary would put me in harm's way, but then again, I didn't know her very well outside of work. Her gaze lifted to meet the camera. One second. Two. The gate slowly opened, the iron screeched in protest as the doors slid across the ground.

"Let's go," she ordered, jogging back to the car.

I stared ahead, unable to take my eyes off the driveway. "Why am I here?"

"All of your questions will be answered once we are inside." Rosemary detected my reluctance and added, "You will be safe here. I promise."

Still not totally convinced, I decided to press on regardless.

Where else can I go?

Dense curtains of green lined the driveway, disrupting the flow of the sun's last rays. Trees stooped low over the car as we passed, and I wondered at the remoteness of this place. The path curved around the overgrowth sharply. I gripped the wheel and decreased the speed of the car, following the inside of the curve while trying to avoid some shrubs that had been crushed by fallen tree limbs. Rosemary seemed unfazed. Truthfully, she looked as if she was entirely in her element – her eyes shone, and her auburn hair was brilliant against the various shades of green outside.

An intimidatingly large house appeared in the midst of the green a few hundred feet away. Several cars were parked to its left.

"Park next to that red Honda." It was the first time Rosemary had spoken since we left the gate.

When I turned the car off, I sighed heavily.

"Ready?" Rosemary asked.

Ready? For what?

"I'm not here as a hostage or anything?" I had to know.

Rosemary snorted. "Of course not."

That wasn't good enough. "So, I can leave whenever I want?"

She tucked an errant lock of hair behind her ear. "Yes."

"Good!" I exclaimed in relief. "Just asking. Doesn't hurt, you know."

I hesitantly climbed out of my car and followed behind Rosemary as we walked toward the house. The air smelled of wet earth and was heavy with the overly sweet scent of lilacs. Many blossoms were planted around the broad porch. There was an opening in the canopy of the trees that allowed the first beams of moonlight to spill over the roof, illuminating the dark wood of the structure. The aged boards groaned under our weight as we walked across them to the front door. There was certainly something fantastical about this place, but I didn't know if that was a good thing or not.

Rosemary faced me and cleared her throat to speak, "I need you to be open-minded and remember that I promised your safety."

I shivered and nodded. I suddenly felt like running, but my body moved separately of my wishes.

The door was unlocked, and Rosemary pushed it open with relative ease. It creaked sonorously in welcome, revealing ornate décor. The effect of its elegance was somewhat diminished by the dim lighting in the house. As we stepped through the entryway, I heard the swelling sounds of chatter. The savory odor of smoke and grilling meat permeated the atmosphere inside and led us to the spacious kitchen situated at the back of the house. All of the appliances were modern – sleek, stainless steel from wall to wall. It must have cost a fortune to complete. Rosemary pointed to the sliding glass doors. Just outside, there were many people crowded around several patio tables eating and socializing.

Rosemary took the lead, allowing me to cross the threshold to the backyard once the doors were opened. All talking ceased. All eyes were on us. I glanced around nervously, my gaze bouncing from face to face. I was searching for anyone familiar to me. I have no clue why. There weren't any kids present, but I counted over thirty adults in attendance. Six were women.

A few men standing at the front of the group puffed their chests, hostile stares dominating their faces. I wanted to leave.

"She is unaware," Rosemary announced calmly.

"What exactly am I unaware of?" I questioned Rosemary quietly, not wanting the others to hear.

A man laughed and emerged from the crowd, walking over to Rosemary and myself. His striking, full cheekbones, almond-shaped eyes, and the earthen tone of his skin were indicative of tribal ancestry. His raven hair was collected into a braid behind his head, which was perched atop wide shoulders and an even wider chest. He towered over everyone around him, but it wasn't his size that made him formidable. There was something in his movements, each one fluid and lending strength to the next. Graceful and primitive.

He smiled, his skin stretching thin across his cheekbones. "I am Tato Sitalo. You must be the woman who causes our—"

"Tato is a good friend of mine. Well, *ours*," Rosemary gestured to everyone outside. "We're all friends. *Family*."

I didn't understand what she meant, but I had a feeling I would come to understand it before the night was over. I met Tato's gaze and said, "Bonnie. Bonnie Collins."

"Where is Rikki?" Rosemary asked Tato, her eyes scanning the group.

"She will come. Soon as she gets over herself." He winked at me. Clearly, there was something I was missing.

Rosemary didn't respond. Instead, she turned to me and put her hand on my shoulder. "Are you hungry?"

I nodded. Recently, I was always hungry.

Tato and Rosemary guided me through the crowd to the grill to grab some burgers and hotdogs. I heaped everything that I could grab on my plate, my stomach growling with each new aroma I encountered.

"Will you be comfortable here for a few minutes alone?" Rosemary stared at the house agitatedly.

I was about to say something when Tato said, "I'll keep her company."

Rosemary's cheeks flushed, and I noticed a tenderness in the curves of her lips I'd never seen before. *Is there something going on between the two of them?* She left us alone together, rushing into the house with great urgency.

Tato took a sip of the beer in his hand. "How long have you known Rosemary?"

I pursed my lips in consideration, trying to remember exactly how long it had been since I first met her. "Almost three years."

Our conversation continued in that vein for several minutes. I appreciated his attempt to make me comfortable, especially since this situation was anything but comfortable. I had an opportunity to survey my surroundings, particularly the people surrounding me. They were uneasy with my presence, that was certain. Rigid bodies framed by equally rigid trees. I couldn't blame them though, I wasn't exactly feeling at home amongst them – they were strangers with strange auras.

"Everything okay?" Rosemary inquired when she returned from the house.

I lowered my voice so only Rosemary would hear and said, "I think I want to go home now."

"I think that is wise," a woman interjected, stepping out of the group and into view. She wore a frown that matched her disdainful tone perfectly.

"Cecilia. She is our guest," Rosemary insisted in attempt to keep the peace.

"I don't care who or *what* she is. She is not welcome here." Cecilia growled, causing Rosemary to take a step back.

I was unused to seeing Rosemary so timid. Her power, like her beauty, was unquestionable. It was unsettling, and I thought about grabbing her hand and running for the door. But I didn't. I was ignorant of the customs of this group. I was loath to make trouble for Rosemary. Well, more trouble than she already appeared to be in with Cecilia. Rosemary's hand found mine and squeezed. I relaxed instantly. She shook her head at me. Once I was calm, the tension in the air diffused a little.

Cecilia muttered under her breath, "We don't need strangers like her, joining our—"

"Cecilia!" A sharp, feminine voice compelled Cecilia and everyone else to silence.

Heads lowered in reverence. The gnawing in my stomach returned. *Oh, my God. It's a cult. This is a cult. Rosemary brought me to the hideout of some crazy cult.*

I peered through the crowd and saw the woman everyone was bowing to – *the woman from the hospital!* The steep angles of her face illuminated by the soft lights of the fire and the moon made her look bold and untamed. As she approached, I noticed that her gait was far willowier than I expected given the sharp edges of her body. The closer she came to me, the more I found myself wanting to put myself in her path.

"Continue." The enchantress waved her hand as she passed me and Rosemary.

Instantly, everything was as before.

Rosemary tucked a stubborn section of her hair behind her ear. "Please, stay and listen, Bonnie."

She gestured for me to follow her, and I did, hoping that she was leading me to the woman who was so captivating. We navigated through the crowd easily enough, stopping when we came to the fireside. Three lawn chairs were facing the flame, the ethereal woman planted in the middle, and two others next to her that were unknown to me. Rosemary nudged me forward. She was going to leave me to do whatever it was she brought me here for completely alone. *Thanks a lot, Rosemary.*

"Are you hungry?" purred the angular seductress.

What was with everyone trying to feed me? This time I wasn't hungry. Could I probably fit more food into me? Sure. But I was too wired to do that. I wanted answers.

"No."

Her eyes analyzed me with terrifying scrutiny. "I apologize for Cecilia's rudeness. She can be quite *animalistic* when it comes to protecting our family."

I wasn't interested in niceties. "Is that what we're calling it? Just ignoring me or saying something petty would have been considered rude. No. That was her being an insecure—"

"Bonnie," Rosemary pleaded from somewhere behind me.

"*Ass*," I finished defiantly.

She should be thankful. I almost called the woman something much worse. I heard someone growl from the direction of where the others sat.

I ignored them and frowned at Rosemary. "She was harsh with you. What kind of friend does that?"

I didn't understand her or this place. If I didn't get a solid amount of information in the next five minutes, I was gone. The entire time I was talking, the woman was watching me as if fascinated. She seemed to be enjoying my attitude.

"Look, I don't care about her. I came here hoping to understand what's happening to me. For some reason, Rosemary wants me to believe you have the answers I need."

"I am sorry about that. This never should have happened."

It was evident that her concern was primarily for her *family*, it was definitely not for me. But I wasn't leaving without an explanation.

"May I ask who you are?"

"Rikki." Sprouts of her coffee-colored hair fell across her forehead and she tried to sweep them away.

"Just Rikki?"

"Rikki Thompson." She smiled, her teeth shining brilliantly in the firelight.

"Bonnie Collins." I pointed at my chest. A useless gesture, I knew.

"I know."

"I'm sure you do."

Rikki's brows arched in amusement rather than surprise. "Do you remember what happened the night you were attacked?"

"Why?"

Rosemary grumbled as if my question was an insult to her. It was a fair question. As far as I was concerned, what happened to me was none of Rikki's business.

"Bonnie! Just answer her question." Rosemary demanded angrily.

"Why?"

Someone from across the yard snorted.

I ignored it.

"No, seriously. Why?" I shook my head in frustration. "I would rather not revisit being ripped apart by a giant wolf, thank you very much."

I was about ready to tear anyone I could reach apart myself. I told my subconscious self not to think so harshly. It wasn't in me to get violent. It certainly wouldn't do any good in this situation. I sensed I was the focus of everyone's attention. Everyone was silent.

"Al-Rikki...you're not seriously considering entrusting *her*? Allowing her to join us?" It was Cecilia who spoke, striding toward us with sober resolve.

Rikki was noticeably irritated. So was I. I glanced at my wristwatch. I was done with this...whatever this was. *I have no clue what I thought I was going to achieve here.* Fortunately, I had a friend here in Mill City. I'd knock on his door and crash on his couch.

"I think I've overstayed my welcome."

"You are free to leave as you please." Rikki sounded disappointed, but I wasn't inclined to care.

"I'll walk her out," Rosemary offered.

Rikki bowed her head slightly in agreement, and I quickly turned on my heel to leave. Rosemary walked with me through the house in silence. I could tell that she didn't want me to go, but I was in no mood to stay where I wasn't welcome and didn't feel comfortable. Everything about that situation was too odd. Once my car was in sight, Rosemary let out a deep breath and stopped walking.

"There's so much you need to know. You will have questions, Bonnie. And when you do, you know where to find me. Just…please call me before next Friday."

That was six days away.

I was done talking. I waved her off dismissively, and then got into my car. Watching her walk back to the house, I shook my head. *What the hell is all of this?*

Chapter Five

I hid in my house for the next three days. I tried to focus on my recovery while getting myself prepared to go back to work. It became easier each day that passed. My body felt stronger – bones hardened, tissue tightened, veins and arteries pumped in a strange, hurried rhythm. Even my vision was sharpened. I put my glasses away in an old shoebox. I questioned whether I should schedule a visit to the doctor, but I decided against it. *What would I even say?*

I felt ready to get out of the house. I went for a run and then stopped at WinCo's to buy a Gatorade. It was a local grocery store that kept all of my favorite snacks in stock. I absently browsed the counter in the deli, intrigued by the selection of prepared foods. I took two pastrami sandwiches, wolfing them down before I made it to the counter to pay. I kept the containers in my hands as I approached the check-out line.

A woman with her toddler and two teenaged boys walked by holding a basket filled with food.

"Mom, please! Can we please get some soda?" The eldest of the two boys begged.

"You ask me one more time and I'm going to take those bags of chips out this basket," she replied.

I smiled at this scene, forgetting myself for a moment.

I didn't notice there was anyone near me until I was forced forward a couple of feet. I turned and shook my arms, wanting to get a look at whoever had bumped into me. It was a man, solidly built. There was no apology. He simply glared at me and then kept walking, as if the entire incident had been my fault. I muttered some obscenities under my breath and then edged closer to the counter. I handed the empty containers to the cashier and then froze. There was something, something that I needed to get to.

Desperate to find whatever was causing me to feel this immediacy, I left my stuff at the register. I sprinted past each aisle until I heard a commotion. Hunger devoured me. My vision blurred. My hands were sweating. I couldn't move. I could smell blood. Rich, sweet blood. It was spilling out from underneath a man who was sitting on the floor, his hand pressed to a wound on his thigh. He was groaning in pain.

He saw me. "A man...he...I don't know what happened."

Somehow, I managed to regain my composure when I saw his distress.

"I'm a paramedic." I spotted the woman with her kids. Her oldest kid was wearing a belt. I pointed to it and shouted, "I need that! Tourniquet!"

He removed it quickly and handed it to me. I secured it above the laceration on his thigh. It was deep, nearly two inches long. As I labored to control the bleeding, I ordered the woman to call 911. I wondered how this happened to him. *A random stabbing? That's really strange.*

I heard the sirens and heaved a sigh of relief. The bleeding was slowing, and I was able to wrap the man's wound in a thick towel supplied to me by a member of the store's staff. There was nothing more I could do, but I kept him calm as the paramedics rushed in to take over. I stood up and stared at my hands. They were painted with blood – it was even under my fingernails. A foreign ache rose in my body from my stomach to my throat. It was burning. Something was off. I stared at my hands a long time.

"I need to wash my hands." I had said it aloud, but I wasn't actually speaking to anyone but myself.

I barely made it into the restroom before I began to fall apart. There was a lot of blood. My mind flashed back to the wolf on top of me and I cringed. Sweat dotted my neck and slid down my back. I was suddenly hot. My eyes burned.

I gritted my teeth and slammed my fist into the mirror. Scared and alone. That's how I felt that night. I never wanted to feel that way again. Hot tears burst free from my eyes, and I ran. Ran out of the restroom and through the crowd of people. My mind dissipated. There was only each movement of my limbs, every flutter of my heart, the sensation of the cool wind against my flesh. I couldn't remember how I got home, but when my mind returned, my body was leaning into the spray of hot water from the showerhead. I immediately thought of Rosemary.

*

I was disappointed to see Rikki at my door when the bell rang. She was holding out an aluminum container of hot tamales in front of her. A peace offering. My mouth watered. Now I didn't care that it was her and not

Rosemary that had come. I stepped aside and gestured for her to come in.

"I know you must be disappointed not to see Rosemary, but I thought it best if I came instead. I wanted to explain. And apologize." She put the container on the coffee table and sat down on the couch, adjusting her position to get comfortable.

I took a seat in the chair across from Rikki. I snatched the container from its place on the table and opened it, greedily gobbling up her peace offering.

Rikki beamed with satisfaction while I ate. "Look, I'm not here to cause you distress. I only want to help you understand what's happening to you."

I set the container down once I had finished. "Okay."

"How about we start with why you texted Rosemary today?" Her hands rested on her kneecaps. She gazed at me intently.

I recounted all that I had experienced since the incident. I watched her as I talked, searching for some change in her demeanor, but she remained motionless and disturbingly calm. Her eyes never left mine. I was certain she would think I was crazy. Any normal person would think so. *Hell, I think I'm acting crazy.* But she kept listening. And part of me knew she would continue to listen and not judge me. I knew that Rosemary wouldn't either. That's why I'd been so drawn to her since waking in the hospital.

When I finished, she relaxed her hands, moving them up to lay atop her thighs. "I have to tell you something."

It was my turn to listen. I worried that I wasn't going to like what I was about to hear.

"This is...difficult, to say the least. I've never been in a position like this." Rikki rose from her spot and began pacing across the living room. Her hands balled into fists and she turned to face me. "Since I first saw you in the hospital, thoughts of you have distracted me."

You could've knocked me over with a feather. "Excuse me?"

She shook her head, almost as if she were trying to discard what she was thinking. She decided on a different approach. She moved closer, kneeling nearly a foot away.

She spoke with sincerity. "Among my family, I am called Alpha."

No. Nope. No. No. No. "I'm not calling you that."

Still kneeling, she continued, "I will be your Alpha and your ma—"

What the hell was she talking about? "I think you need to leave. This…whatever the hell this is…well, it's a little too much for me."

She stood, a pained expression on her face. "Perhaps it should have been Rosemary that came here today. I-I am not myself and I don't think I can explain things very well right now. Please, allow Rosemary to bring you to my house again tonight."

I was still in a state of confusion over what had just transpired, but I couldn't go any longer without answers. "What about your groupies?"

Rikki snorted. "They will keep their distance."

"Then I'll be there. But I expect a clear explanation about what's happening to me. After that, we can revisit this whole *Alpha* thing.

Her smile was sincere. "I'll be waiting."

Chapter Six

"I'm glad you decided to come."

I shut my eyes and faced the window in response.

Rosemary was seeking to fill the unpleasant silence that pervaded the air inside the car. It was the first time either of us had spoken since she picked me up at my house after I had spent the better part of the last few hours arguing with myself about whether I should text her or even continue down this insane path. I had written several drafts of texts that I planned to send, but I ended up deleting them all. Ultimately, I ended up calling her. She was at my front door not long afterwards.

Letting Rosemary take me back to that house and those people did not mean that I wanted to be involved with their *family*. The only reason I was returning to that den of weirdos was to finally get the answers I needed. I had to know what was happening to me. I had to. I also had to find out what exactly was the deal with Rikki. She was stranger than the others, and her visit left a bad taste in my mouth. I had no clue what she was after, and nothing she said to me made sense.

"Something is clearly bothering you." Rosemary's fingers tightened around the steering wheel. Something was bothering her too.

"Besides the obvious?" I replied dryly. "I'm not exactly looking forward to this, and you know that."

"I'm sorry, but it *will* get better. You'll understand once you hear what we have to say." Her voice was gentle. She reached over the center console and touched my arm gingerly. "Relax."

She would make a great mother.

I smiled, but not without reservation.

The longer we drove the more nervous I became. I couldn't be sure how my life would change after tonight. I wasn't even sure I wanted it to change. But it would, so there was no point in resisting. I opened my eyes and watched the scenery transform as we drove – the beautiful green of the landscape was swallowed up with the black, grey, and blue hues of night. The shadows falling across the road conjured the memory of the incident that had started everything. Those yellow eyes were ever with me. I shuddered.

"Bonnie. We are here." Rosemary's honeyed voice pierced the silence once more.

The familiar grounds did nothing to allay my misgivings. There were less cars in the driveway tonight, which was a little comforting. *The smaller the audience, the better this will be.* There could be nothing worse than doing this with a large group of people who hated me.

Stepping out the car, I immediately noticed Rikki and Tato standing on the porch together. They were deep in conversation, and from the looks of it, it was something grave. Both of their postures were rigid, almost as if they were statues. If I hadn't seen their lips moving as they spoke, the image of them on the porch could have fooled anyone into believing they were clay sculptures. I leaned against the car. There was no way I was going to interrupt this conversation.

Rikki caught sight of Rosemary and me from the porch. Only her head turned, her body didn't move. "You should take Rosemary."

Tato scowled. His gaze remained fixed on Rikki.

"She has a good sense of things," Rikki stressed. "You know it too."

Tato scoffed. He shot an annoyed look at Rosemary. "I like to hunt alone."

Rikki took hold of his arm. Tato winced and then lowered his head, but Rikki kept her grip firm. "You *will* take her with you."

Tato grunted in surrender, and Rikki released his arm.

I was struck with the realization that I was going to be alone with Rikki. *Great.* I watched as Tato practically vaulted off the porch and sprinted toward the tree line without pausing to allow Rosemary to catch up to him. She chuckled, and then gave chase, disappearing into the thick brush. Neither of them had weapons when they left, nor were they remotely dressed for hunting in this cool weather. *This is too weird.* I wanted to leave. I definitely wasn't ready for this much weird.

"You are free to leave at any time," Rikki remarked.

Somehow, that didn't sound so reassuring. I combed my fingers through my hair agitatedly. I scratched my jawline and stared vacantly at the spot where Rosemary and Tato vanished. I wanted to avoid looking at Rikki for as long as I could, but I simply couldn't look away for too long. I was drawn in by her presence, and the intriguing slopes of her body. Even though I still didn't like being in this place or the general attitude of the *family,* I could at least enjoy looking at Rikki while we were left alone together.

Deciding not to delay the inevitable, I strode over to Rikki and she led me behind the house to a small shed almost completely hidden by the trees. The gnawing sensation in my gut resurfaced as I scanned the chipped paint and the rotted boards of the structure. Surprisingly, the door made no noise when she pulled it back to reveal a converted studio apartment. I gasped audibly. It was beautiful – a picture utterly contrary to its outer appearance.

A kitchenette was the first thing I saw as we walked through the doorway. To the right, a retro couch hugged the wall next to a small dining table surrounded by three chairs. A flat screen was mounted on the wall over an electric fireplace facing the couch. Toward the back of the shed was a decent-sized bed that had a comforter with a colorful pattern.

"This is where you sleep?" I asked with genuine amazement. I was also a bit curious as to why she didn't sleep in the house.

She nodded.

This cozy place didn't match the demanding and stiff woman standing in front of me. This place looked as if it belonged to a bubbly socialite, not this angular seductress who was studying my movements closely.

"Hard to picture me in here?" she asked, but I believed she already knew the answer to her own question.

"Do you really need to ask?" I grinned. "But why the shed? Why not the house?"

"The house belongs to my family. Here, I am not disturbed." Rikki closed the door and walked to the modest refrigerator. "Would you like something to drink? Anything to eat?"

A Night Claimed

I plopped down on the couch. "Just something to drink."

Rikki took a glass canister from the refrigerator and set it out on the counter. She then retrieved two cups from the cabinet and filled each cup with the contents of the canister. Sauntering over to me, cups in hand, I noticed the smoothness of her skin for the first time.

She handed me the cup and I took a sip. "Mmm, I love cold tea. This is really good."

"Brewed it myself. I like using my own ingredients," she explained as she sipped idly.

I straightened in my place as I watched how her lips brushed against the cup as drank. It was quiet save for the distant chirping of crickets. Rikki was stunning, to be sure, and I was beginning to see the softness in her edges. The silence between us wasn't awkward, but I needed to talk. I needed the answers for which I returned to this house.

"Listen, thank you for the hospitality, but you know that I didn't come here with you and sip tea."

She clicked her tongue and narrowed her eyes at me, suddenly serious. "How wild is your imagination?"

"If you told me now that you saw a mermaid once, I'd be inclined to believe you." I tapped the side of my cup. "Have you seen one?"

She took a sip of her tea. "Unfortunately, I have not. They have been extinct for some time. Sorry."

Not sure whether to take Rikki's comment as a joke, I left it alone. I put my cup down on the little table next to the couch. "I'm in no mood for games or cryptic questions. I want to know what's happening to me."

Rikki bit her lip. "It's not so easy to say, and it's certainly not easy to know."

My hands balled into fists in my lap. "I don't care! Ever since I was attacked, nothing has been right. Nothing has been the same. I came here because Rosemary told me that there were people who could help me, and so far, I've only been getting jerked around. It's enough! Now, tell me what I need to know."

Rikki's hand reached out and brushed my cheek, catching me off guard. When her thumb grazed the corner of my mouth, I tried not to bite her finger. She was sexy and for a split-second, I forgot I was supposed to be angry. I squeezed my thighs together.

"You had something at the corner of your mouth," she said, her gaze still lingering on my lips.

"Oh." That was all I could say.

I was failing at keeping my composure. I licked my bottom lip when her hand moved away. She watched me.

"What is this?" I asked softly.

"What do you want it to be?"

I wasn't going to answer that. "I thought I was coming here for the truth."

"You are learning the truth," Rikki said, then took another sip of tea.

It was hard to do, but I finally pulled my eyes away from the trap of her mesmerizing gaze. I looked around, taking a deep breath. While I was doing that, a thought popped into my head.

"Is this a date?" I asked, only half-serious.

Her hazel eyes locked with my own. "This–"

A desperate shriek tore through the night air and Rikki rushed out of the shed and into the black of the night.

Chapter Seven

The front door of the house was open. Visceral cries emanated from its center, echoing down the network of hallways. I hurried behind Rikki, my heart thumping wildly against my ribcage. I had no idea what we would discover when we arrived in the living room, but I especially wasn't prepared to encounter Rosemary lying naked on the floor, the skin of her leg buried beneath soupy webs of blood. Tato was kneeling near her shoulder stroking her matted hair. Another person I didn't recognize was crouched near her stomach, his hands grasping hers.

"Damn it!" the unfamiliar man bellowed. "I don't think we can get it out."

"Rosemary," Rikki whispered tremulously.

"Move," I barked, my paramedic instincts kicking in.

Tato and the stranger looked at me and then to Rikki, who said nothing. Her eyes scanned Rosemary's wound and anger flickered across her face. The two men moved away from Rosemary but remained in the room. She shivered as beads of sweat formed at her pores. Her eyes were closed.

"Are there any medical supplies here?" I looked to everyone in the room for an answer.

I heard someone leave the room. My attention remained on Rosemary. It was difficult to see her in this state. I mean, I was always sympathetic to the suffering of those I treated, but lately it had become harder to deal with the pain of others. It was much worse with Rosemary. I lightly brushed her cheek with my fingers.

The stranger reappeared with supplies. I ripped through them in the space of a heartbeat and retrieved what I needed. Once I managed to wipe away some of the blood from the site of the wound, it became clear it was caused by a gunshot.

"Call 911." I went straight to work tending to her injury.

No one moved.

Carefully, I slid my finger inside the broken tissue to locate the bullet. Not an action generally performed in the field, but the unwillingness of the others to call for help told me that I was alone in my efforts. The bullet lodged itself not far from the surface of her skin. No artery was severed. I breathed a sigh of relief. I moved with renewed determination, wanting to get the bullet out as quickly as possible without causing Rosemary any unnecessary pain. My index finger trailed along its smooth surface. In one swift motion, I pulled it from her thigh and let it drop on the floor next to me.

Rosemary leapt up as if she had awoken from a nightmare. I grabbed her shoulders firmly, pushing her down against the floor as she struggled against me. She snarled and thrashed, tufts of her tangled hair escaping the glue of the sweat covering her face.

No one moved.

What the hell?

I screamed, "Did anyone call for an amb—"

"No," Rikki replied shrilly.

"She was shot!" I was nearing to the point of hysteria. Rosemary continued to fight my grip.

Tato cursed and wiped his hand across his mouth. "I should have gone alone."

"If you had, it would be *you* injured instead. Except, *you* would be in the forest bleeding out alone," Rikki reprimanded angrily.

Tato grumbled and stormed out of the room.

Rosemary freed herself from my arms and sprinted through the open door and out into the blackness. I stood ready to follow her, but Rikki grabbed my arm, preventing me from leaving.

I yanked my arm away and shoved her with as much strength as I could muster. "Don't touch me!"

"You can't take her to the hospital," she said matter-of-factly.

"Rosemary is my friend! Colleague. Whatever! I won't let her die because of whatever twisted shit is going on here!"

"How can *she* want you?" Rikki snarled, moving closer to my face. She looked conflicted.

What the hell is she talking about?"

I didn't care. I cared about Rosemary and I had to get to her before she bled to death. "I'm taking Rosemary out—"

Rikki flung my body against the wall as effortlessly as if I were a doll made of cotton.

"She is *my* wolf!" An inhuman voice growled. It came from Rikki.

As I turned to face her, I watched as Rikki's eyes transformed from hazel to a milky amber. I inhaled sharply, a million thoughts racing through my mind. *That couldn't...I must be seeing things.* But they were still there. I knew I had to get out of the house. There was a pen on the end table beside us. I grabbed it and jammed it into her outer thigh. Rikki howled and freed me to rid her thigh of the intrusive item.

I scampered outside of the house in the direction I had seen Rosemary disappear. A small group was standing in a circle in the backyard, their eyes focused on something on the ground in the center. I couldn't see what they were looking at, but something inside me urged me to get to the middle of the circle. I moved quickly, shoving immobile bodies aside as I made my way forward. The thudding of my heart was so loud I was certain that everyone else could hear it.

It was Rosemary. She was crouched on the ground, thick hair sprouting from her body in dense patches. Her slender frame writhed, bending in grotesque fashion. Bones cracked and reformed. Sinew bubbled and burst, and virgin tendon sprang forth, enveloping Rosemary's form underneath the multiplying fur. I couldn't move.

No. No. No. Fuck no. No. No.

Vomit gurgled in the pit of my abdomen and threatened to rise. *This cannot be happening. This is impossible. There's no way.* I tried willing my body to move, to run, to scream, to do anything at all, but I was frozen in place as this feral metamorphosis neared its end.

I staggered, relieved to have movement returned to me. Something wet and hot slid across my face. I turned and found myself facing Rikki once again.

She held out Rosemary's car keys in the space between us. "Do not run."

*

A Night Claimed

It was early the next morning when someone knocked on my bedroom door. I grabbed my phone to check the time. It was barely eight in the morning.

"Yeah?" I groaned in resistance as I stretched.

"You have a visitor."

Damn it.

"Um, okay."

I grappled with myself for a minute or two about what to do. I knew I would have to come out of the bedroom, but I had no idea who was waiting for me. It could be Rosemary. If it was, she certainly wasn't here in the form of a giant wolf. I could easily imagine my roommates' reaction to seeing a wolf at the door, but I doubted that a wolf would simply ring a doorbell, though. If I was gambler however, I'd put all my money on it being Rikki. She was too much of a control freak to let this whole thing slide without talking to me about it.

I put on my pajama pants, feeling nervous as hell. I was still mad at her. But not quite as much as before. It made sense now why Rikki didn't want to take Rosemary to the hospital. I'd been thinking hard on what this all meant. Did a little research. I surprised myself in not thinking I was crazy. Apparently, it would take much more than that to force me into a psychiatrist's office.

Rikki was standing in my doorway with a container of food. She held it out to me. "Please."

I made no attempt to conceal my displeasure at finding her at my front door. I raised my index finger in the air. "You say one thing I don't like, just one, and you are out."

"I understand." She bit her lip and dropped her gaze but kept her offering out in the space between us.

My roommates smiled and passed the two of us in the doorway. They had to work.

Rikki followed me into the living room, and I gestured for her to sit. She chose the couch, lowering herself with the mesmerizing grace of a practiced geisha. I proceeded to plunk myself down in the chair across from her. I wanted as much distance between us as possible. I'd spent the last few days wrestling with everything that I witnessed while in this otherworldly creature's company. That's what she was – what all of them were. A group of werewolves. I felt the urge to retch for the umpteenth time since I saw Rosemary *change.*

The *pop* of aluminum packaging reminded me that I wasn't alone. Rikki was creating dents in the bottom half of the container with her perfectly-polished fingernails.

I cleared my throat. *Let's get this over with.* "What do you want?"

"I am sorry for last night. It wasn't the way you deserved to find out."

How exactly is the right way to find out that things that are supposed to be fairytales are real?

Her coffee-colored hair rushed forward as she lowered her head. "I am also sorry for my actions last night."

I wondered if she practiced that line in the mirror. It seemed rehearsed. "Can you specify?"

Pop. "The comments I made."

"The comments you made?" I repeated, trying to dissect her words as if they concealed some deeper meaning. "Screw your comments. How about apologizing for slamming me against the freaking wall?" I flung my arm out toward the wall behind me for emphasis.

Rikki frowned. "You were threatening to take my wolf."

"Excuse me? Rosemary is not *your* wolf. She is a...person. I think." I didn't sound too confident, but I was not going to recant my statement. "And if you would have explained yourself—"

"I don't owe you any explanation," she snarled, her body stiffened. "I am her Alpha. It is my duty to protect her from any who could cause her harm."

It was nearly impossible to ignore her implication that I was somehow a threat to Rosemary. "Why are you even here? Clearly, you have no intention of making amends."

With an exaggerated huff, Rikki rolled her eyes. "You forced your way into our business and then didn't like it when things didn't go your way."

"Oh, my freaking goodness. She was shot!" I shouted.

After a few deep breaths, I discovered that Rikki was staring at me. Her body was no longer stiff. Maybe she was trying to calm herself as well.

"You put me in that position. I helped her. Don't treat me like an inconvenience. Like someone who didn't care."

I was stressed and scared. I didn't know what any of this meant. I feared the worse. I only wanted answers, even if those answers were going to make me crazy. I squeezed my eyes shut against the onset of tears, not wanting to cry in front of this woman. I rubbed my eyes.

Rikki set the container on the coffee table with an audible *thud*. "Look, I know that you care about Rosemary, but there are things you haven't learned yet about the dynamics of a pack. I am her Alpha, and it is my duty to protect her and all of those who belong to our family."

Pack. Alpha. The words hovered like storm clouds between the two of us. The more I heard, the more I experienced…all of it was working overtime to ensure that I couldn't dismiss any of it. It was real. Too real. Nevertheless, I wasn't ready to concede to Rikki when it came to Rosemary.

"Well, you don't know anything about the dynamics of *my* friendship with Rosemary. She was shot. Bleeding out! I wasn't going to stand there gawking at her. I am a trained professional and I could help her, so I did."

There was a sharp pain in my chest. I realized I had forgotten to breathe for a few moments. I inhaled deeply, but I couldn't calm myself. There were too many conflicting emotions swirling around under my skin. Rikki sat unmoving. Her stoic demeanor left no morsels for interpretation. I shifted in the chair. She watched. *This is infuriating.*

"Are you ever going to tell me if Rosemary is all right?"

A smile threatened to form at the corners of her lips, but she subdued it. "She is fine."

I scratched at the skin above my ear impatiently. "I'm having trouble dealing with all of this. I mean, any *normal person* would have trouble with this. Wolves. Werewolves. I'm not crazy. And the wolf that attacked me…was it…did it belong—"

"Whoever attacked you did not belong to me."

I nodded, not sure how I felt about that constant, possessive tone of hers.

"So, Rosemary isn't the only one who can turn into a wolf? Cecilia too?" I asked.

Rikki nodded.

Great. Cecilia could literally rip me apart. Here I was provoking a wolf in woman's clothing. I laced my fingers together on top of my lap and stared at my fingernails.

"Ask it."

Am I that obvious?

"Are you a wolf too?"

She nodded again.

"God." I covered my face with my hands. "Wolf. It's not every day you meet people who can turn into wolves." I laughed at the absurdity of this whole situation.

Rikki kept her eyes on me. She sat in silence, as if she knew I wasn't finished.

"I mean, in movies or books. This is where this kind of stuff belongs. Wolves. People turning into wolves." I laughed so hard I started to cry.

Rikki's soft smile stared back at me.

"Gosh." I pinched the skin of my bottom lip between two fingers. "Wolf. Werewolf."

Rikki was motionless. A statue peering back at me. I wondered if she understood how I was feeling.

"Okay," I rubbed my thighs nervously, "so, is it like the movies…or…?"

She chuckled and her coffee-colored tresses bounced against her shoulders. "The movies get some things right, but a lot of it is pure fantasy."

She had my attention.

"What is the truth?"

"Well, the basic things you're probably familiar with are true, like the pack hierarchy, the involuntary shift under the full moon, and enhanced skills and tempers."

She stopped and thought for a moment, chewing on the inside of her lip. She then added, "There is one thing that people assume about werewolves that is entirely wrong: we don't have a human lifespan. We actually live for a very long time."

I leaned forward in my seat, my fingers gripping the edge of the chair. "How long are we talking?"

Rikki's grin spread wide across her cheeks. "Centuries."

Centuries. I gulped. "How old are you?"

Her expression didn't change. It's possible that she expected my question. "I was born in 1610 in Jamestown, Virginia."

Oh my God. She was born in the first settlement! My world was changing too fast and I wasn't sure that I keep up. "Do you have any Native American ancestry?"

Those wide, steep cheekbones of hers couldn't have come from Europe.

"Half," she replied coolly.

"You aren't related to Pocahontas, by any chance?" I couldn't help myself.

Rikki snickered playfully. "Not at all. But I did meet her once. Maybe twice."

I hadn't expected that. "What—"

"I need you to understand something right now – this is not an easy life. I have seen many perish in my own lifetime. It is especially difficult for those who are turned."

"Turned? So, you weren't born?"

"No. Werewolf births are rare these days. Our numbers have been dwindling since the English first came to this country. They slaughtered so many."

Her grief was evident in the slight trembling of her chin. She shook her head and the tremble vanished. I thought of the years that Rikki had lived – the things she must have seen. It was both extraordinary and terrifying. No wonder she seemed so unflappable.

Rikki's expression altered instantly. Sympathy. "Listen, if I have been a bit severe, it was not my intention. I did not have a mentor to guide me – I was alone. As a child who had mixed ancestry, I wasn't accepted by anyone already. Add to that a supernatural aspect…well…I'm sure you can imagine what that must have been like."

"What are you trying to say to me?"

"Perhaps this is enough for today." Rikki reached for the container on the table.

I was not ready to stop. "Please, keep going. I want…I *need* to know everything."

Rikki's hands returned to her lap in defeat. "All right. Well, you should know that as a pack we follow certain laws that are meant for our protection. Some laws vary from pack to pack, but most are the same. The wolf who attacked you was not part of any pack. It was a rogue."

My brows furrowed. "Rogue?"

"Yes. From what we can tell, this wolf has been attacking others, attempting to create some sort of loyal army."

"An army. But why?"

Rikki shrugged. "We don't know yet. Control of territory, maybe."

I nodded in understanding. "The night I was attacked. There was a man. I was trying to help him."

"A classic trap. A good Samaritan…" Rikki paused and looked me straight in the eyes.

"Dumb enough to stop, right?" I knew I had been foolish that night. Hearing her say it would not make a difference.

"You are who you are."

"And who is that?" I asked, curious to know what she thought of me.

"Sympathetic. Intuitive to others needs. That is a strength," Rikki averred. For some reason, it meant a lot to hear her say that. "I am sorry that you were hurt. That all of this happened to you."

"I almost died." My fingernails dug into the fabric of my pajama bottoms.

Suddenly, I realized what this revelation meant for me. I was supposed to become a drone in a rogue's army. My life was turned upside-down without my consent. Tears flooded my eyes. Maybe to someone else it would be a privilege, but I had no choice. I made no decision. Someone made it for me for their own selfish gain.

I blew air between my lips forcefully and stared intensely at the carpet, as if it had all the answers I needed. "W-will I…turn?"

Her hand found mine and squeezed. "Friday night when the moon reaches its peak, you will turn."

It was not a matter of *if* but *when*. And that *when* was in a day and a half. Hot tears left their trails on my cheeks. I was scared and unsure of my future, the events of this past week, and how Rosemary, Rikki, and her entourage were acting. It made sense but that didn't make it easy to accept. Only a few minutes ago, I was resisting her protective and possessive arms. Now, I cried into them. This is not what I wanted.

"What about my life?" I sniffled. I pressed my face into her shoulder. Her arms were tight around me.

"You can still have a life," Rikki whispered. "It will only take time to adjust."

I started to worry about my job, my family, my friends. Could things continue with any of it? Could things possibly find a comfortable normality? Could I endure the sight of blood without becoming crazed?

"I-*we* will all teach you how to control your wolf," Rikki said.

Is that what Rosemary does in the emergency room? Control her *wolf?*

"I don't do...big groups." I distanced myself from her embrace.

She did not try to keep me in her arms. "It is difficult being this way, and the pack is the best support system you could have, especially right now. It is rare for a woman werewolf to be a rogue. You'd have to be twice as strong to survive and to live well."

"Are you saying I can't be alone?" The thought of her telling me I had no choice was infuriating. I wanted control in my life, especially after the attack.

"In this instance, yes. I was once a rogue. But I had no other option. It's an impossible path to walk. Each time I encountered another werewolf, I had to fight for my life. You will always be expected to be part of a pack or someone's mate. Women werewolves must work twice as hard to survive by themselves. Your world isn't the only one that is patriarchal."

"But you are an Alpha and a woman!"

"True. But in order for that to happen I had to kill the last Alpha. I have been challenged since then, but I have remained Alpha for 20 years. As far as I know, I am the only female Alpha of this era. I've only ever met one other female Alpha. I was much younger then. And she no longer lives." I started to say something, but Rikki wasn't finished. "My pack. Well, most of my pack, respects me. But I know, secretly, some are waiting for me to show a weakness. A few others don't believe I will last long. Some like Cecilia. She is proud to have a woman as an Alpha but fears I won't last. That is why she is threatened by you."

"How come?"

"Because of your presence, I have now shown weakness. You. I am drawn to you as a mate and I feel the need to protect you."

I pretended I didn't hear her. I didn't know what to think about what she said. Mate. Strange word in a strange, new world. Being an Alpha's mate sounded too serious and important. Bigger even than marriage. It was not something I could consider in my present state of mind.

"And…you are becoming an Omega."

She lost me.

"It is rare to find an Omega. And the few who do exist in this decade are threatened, or even killed. It is hard to have an Omega in a pack."

"Why?"

"You can make a dominant become submissive around you. Not that a dominant could be 100 percent submissive, but they are certainly more malleable and less aggressive. Omegas are the heart and soul of any pack they join. You will not be submissive nor dominant. You will be protective of those who are in your pack and others who are weaker or stronger. You do not bow to the power of an Alpha and could easily slip through the magic that forces you to shift by an Alpha's command. There is so much more you will learn. But that is another reason Cecilia and a few others are threatened by you."

"What does this all mean? For me?" I looked down at my fingers once again, trying desperately to avoid her gaze.

Rikki lifted my chin, forcing my eyes to meet hers. "You will challenge everything I say or do."

"Only if it sounds ridiculous."

"You've been human for 28 years. Anything I tell you from here on out will sound ridiculous to you."

"Then get ready and good luck." I willed my nerves into a calm. "Does this mean I will stop being human?"

"I have human attributes. We look human. But, no. Once you are werewolf you are no longer human."

"All I really needed was a *yes* or *no*." It felt as if the ground under me had slipped away. I didn't know how to be anything else other than what I had always been. I was Bonnie. Who was I now?

Rikki stood. "Rosemary will pick you up in the morning."

I frowned. "Why exactly?"

"The full moon's tomorrow night. You can't be here when that happens."

I knew she was right, but I wasn't thrilled that yet again, I had no choice. Suppressing the urge to scream and thrash and cry was a herculean task. Rikki headed for the door, successfully evading my ire. At least, for the moment.

She turned to face me when her hand turned the knob of the door. "No. You have no choice. And if I must come and drag your ass to the pack home, I will."

"Asshole!" I shouted at the door after she had disappeared.

Chapter Eight

"How long do you plan to stay out here? It's been over two hours."

"I'm a medic. We spend up to 14 hours in a rig at a time. I can hold out," I grumbled, my gazed fixed on the dashboard.

Rikki slapped the doorframe exasperatedly. "Damn it, Bonnie! You can't afford to be weak the first time you shift! You need to eat and hydrate."

"You know what I've concluded?" I crossed my arms across my chest in protest. "Besides some minor changes, I feel the same. You could be wrong. I think you're wrong."

Rikki sighed and her arms fell to her sides. "Bonnie."

"No!" I snapped. I shook my head angrily. "I'm still just me. I-I can't be anything else. My career, my family, my friends. Me. You have embraced being a werewolf, but it's not for me."

Rikki leaned her head against the door of Rosemary's car. "Bonnie, you *will* shift."

I tried not to cry. I bit my lip, but the tears came anyway. I wiped them away as they formed and fell. I had time to prepare for this day, but I still wasn't ready. I still couldn't believe it – process it. Even when Rosemary arrived to fetch me this afternoon, I pretended that I had no idea what she was talking about. It was childish, I knew. It was also futile. This change was racing toward me at a breakneck pace, and there was absolutely nothing I could do to stop it from happening.

"Come inside," she pleaded. "Please, Bonnie. This is not something that you can do alone."

I snorted. "You say a few sweet words and I'm supposed to succumb to your demands?"

"You know what…" Rikki yanked me out of the car before I could fight back. She lifted me over her shoulder as easily as if I was the size of a small toddler, and then she carried me toward the shed.

"Fuck. Damn it!" I bellowed. "Seriously, Rikki!"

I punched her in the back a few times, then stopped when I heard a loud growl. I let my body go limp when I spotted Tato on the front porch. He smiled and waved at the both of us, and then disappeared inside the main house.

Rikki dropped me on her couch and walked into the kitchen.

"Are you freaking insane?"

"No," Rikki said. She handed me a cup of water.

I drained the cup in a few gulps. She refilled the cup and I emptied it immediately. A third cup was offered, but I was satisfied.

Someone knocked on the front door.

"What?" she snarled.

Whoever was on the other side of the door didn't enter. He just said, "Don't know if you noticed, but there's a fight breaking out. Thought you should know."

"Damn it." She pointed her index finger at me. "Wait here."

I scoffed at the closed door. She was naïve to think I would listen.

But if I thought I was just going to waltz into the main house without issue, I was mistaken. As soon as I opened the door to the shed, Tato's grinning face was the first thing to greet me.

"Alpha told me to make sure you don't leave."

Apparently, Rikki wasn't naïve. I groaned. "I am not going to leave. I only want to see what's going on."

"I'm sure."

"Honest."

Tato studied me, then nodded. "Fine. But I will be right on your tail."

I glared at him, but I knew when I was defeated. We walked to the house together, Tato a few paces behind me. There were more people inside the main house than I had ever seen before, but they did not linger. Most were making their way to the backyard where Rikki was standing between two men. They were both taller than her, but their heads bowed so low they almost appeared small.

"This is your fault," Cecilia gladly pointed out. She stood to my side, opening the sliding door wider. "Your fucking mood swings have been causing everyone anxiety. That rogue should have killed you."

Rikki was in front of Cecilia in a flat second. She snarled, causing Cecilia to drop to her knees.

"Toni?" I barely recognized Rikki's voice. "Get your mate and remind her to stay away from mine."

I was about to say I wasn't her mate. However, my instinct warned me not to say anything. No matter how conflicted I was, I didn't want to undermine her authority in this pack. Something told me that Rikki's position was more important than my feelings right now. We would have this conversation privately.

Rikki took hold of my hand and pulled me behind her. I knew we were headed back to the shed. Rosemary flashed me a sheepish grin as we passed. Once we were back in her shed, Rikki paced the length the floor. She was upset. That was obvious. I stood there watching her wondering what I should say. We hadn't known each other for long, but I had a feeling that despite her rough and possessive personality, she had a fragile heart.

My hand on her shoulder was enough to make her stop pacing. "I'm sorry. I am not making this easy for you or your pack…of people."

Rikki shook her head. "It isn't you. I should have handled this better."

"No matter how many years you've lived there will always be something that happens to teach you something new."

Rikki sucked her bottom lip into her mouth. "Thank you for not challenging me."

"I will collect on that favor later," I grinned playfully.

She smiled. "Are you ready to finally join the pack?"

"Join the pack?" I questioned, a little taken aback by her frankness.

"As in, join the pack in the house," she clarified. "I know you have no interest in becoming one of my wolves."

I grimaced. I had no desire to be treated as property.

Rikki gritted her teeth. "I think you should try to make friends with everyone. I don't see you as being anti-social…so try to think about it that way."

She was upset. I think I had offended her with my reaction. I said nothing, but I nodded, and then she guided me back to the main house.

A Night Claimed

*

"Want another burger?" Rosemary asked, handing me a second burger before I could reply.

Dreaming of those yellow eyes prompted a feverish hunt for the beast as soon as my own eyes opened this afternoon. It wasn't there. I was beginning to wonder if the nightmare was only about the attack, and not also about how I was dreading the change in my life. I checked my arms and legs for any signs of mushrooming wolf hair obsessively for the next hour. Occasionally, I'd examine my teeth. The only thing that seemed to be changing was my temperature – it was rising at a steady rate.

The sky was a bright mixture of orange and red. Blackness threatened the horizon. No one mentioned the fight that had called Rikki from the shed earlier. They appeared to be more concerned with devouring as much food as possible, probably trying to amass a great amount of energy before shifting tonight.

I accepted the hamburger from Rosemary, realizing that I would need to do the same as the pack. "Sure."

I mostly sat alone while I ate. The other pack members were uneasy in my presence, and I could hardly blame them. My feelings about the upcoming change were perfectly plain from the start. I nibbled on the burger thoughtfully. I was still unsure if this was what I wanted.

"Everyone is eating at the tables." Rosemary pointed behind her as she sat beside me on a lawn chair.

"I'm fine here," I insisted.

Rosemary shifted in the seat. "I know we've only ever been colleagues, but I want that to change. Not everyone here has given you the best impression, I know. We have to change this though, because we are going to be family."

"You don't have to explain—"

"No," Rosemary continued adamantly. "Let me try. They are my pack, for better or worse. And I love them. We laugh and go out together. We help heal each other wounds, physically and emotionally. And yes, some antagonize you and have their own views that you will never agree with, but that's family."

"I have nothing against that," I snapped hotly.

"Why don't you tell Rikki how you are feeling right now? Your anxiety about tonight?"

I furrowed my brows. "Why?"

"Maybe she will understand, and if she does, the others will too."

I stood, my jaw set, my burger unfinished. "I don't need understanding. I just don't belong, and they know it. So, why pretend otherwise?"

"They're wrong," Rosemary asserted. "You're wrong."

Anger flooded my veins, settling somewhere between my heart and lungs. "Look, I still think this is all crazy. There is no proof I will turn into one of *you*. No facts. And the sooner we get this night over with, the sooner I can go back home and pretend this night never happened. I can go back to my life."

Our conversation was attracting the attention of the others, but I didn't care. I was already halfway to the back door of the house.

"Bonnie!" Rosemary shouted. "You cannot leave!"

I ignored her and was almost to the door when Rikki jumped in front of me, blocking my path.

If it wasn't clear that I was upset earlier, it was fairly evident now.

"You and your family barely tolerate me. Don't act like you care all of a sudden. Move!" I yelled.

My gums throbbed, and the fluids in my stomach churned. I caught sight of my reflection in the glass of the door and froze. My eyes were no longer brown but gold. A gold so bright that it could light the way in the night. *No! No! This can't be happening!* I lowered my head and shoved Rikki aside to run into the house.

I found a bathroom and locked myself inside, squeezing my body between the toilet and wall. Fugitive sobs fled my throat. I was scared. I didn't want this. I wanted to be normal. I wanted to live my life how I'd been living it since I was born. Instead, I was trapped in a house with werewolves who hated me. And now, I was becoming one of them. All I could think about was how my life would change. Could I eat my favorite donuts? Could I keep my job? Would I lose anyone that mattered to me? Would I go rogue and attack someone? Would anyone ever like me for being a strange kind of werewolf? Being an Omega sounded like a lonely existence. Did it hurt to shift? Would I ever accept what I was now turning into?

There were too many questions, and I was terrified of the answers.

There was a knock at the bathroom door. My head shot upward, tears still spilling out of my eyes. I wanted to be alone. I said nothing.

"I'm going to come in," Rikki advised softly.

"The door's—"

The door opened. She stepped in, closing it behind her. "It doesn't lock. Can I sit?"

I shrugged. "Why not?"

My eyes were probably red and puffy. *What a great look.*

"Are my eyes...?" I pulled my knees closer to my chin.

Rikki put her hand on my shoulder, her eyes on mine. "They have returned to their natural brown."

I sniffled and returned her gaze. Even at a time like this, I couldn't help but notice how close she was to me, or how the heat from her hand seared my skin. I had quickly grown accustomed to the angles of her body and her brusque manner. I knew I could cry in front of her. So, I did.

"You will see that your wolf will reflect who you are now."

I snorted. "Come on, Rikki. I'm going to be different."

I tried to pretend I wasn't sexually frustrated with her hand on me. I wanted to give in to her touch but was too stubborn to let her know how I felt, as though I was submitting to her dominant personality.

"Yes and no," she said without hesitation. "You will develop stronger personality traits. But...that sarcasm of yours will remain. So will your stubbornness and your desire to help others."

"Okay." I believed her. It was scary, but I did.

"I'm hard to understand. And complicated. You don't know whether to punch me or..." Rikki smiled. "Give us a chance. Get to know me. You will see, we are more alike than you think. I am yours, if you want me."

She was being serious. I couldn't stop thinking about our complex and unique relationship. She was mysterious with eyes I could fall into for hours at a time. Exotic and alluring. Rough in the sexiest way. She was a woman not often seen in this world. But she stirred me. I wanted her, to touch her, and to claim her. Show her off to the world as mine.

Where in the world did all of that come from? It was as if someone else was occupying my mind, communicating through me its affection for Rikki.

Rikki watched me as my fingertips traced the line of her jaw. She inhaled sharply when my fingertips trailed down her neck to her collarbone.

"Let me see how I can manage being..." it was hard saying the words. I observed my hands moving of their own volition, returning to her jaw. "If I can handle being different first. Then, I think taking you on will be easy."

Rikki snorted playfully. "You think so?"

I giggled. "Maybe."

Her expression was serious. "You *will* get through this and then you will realize that being a werewolf is a blessing. It took me a hundred years to learn that. You'll learn it a lot sooner."

Cecilia knocked on the door. "Pack's waiting."

I sniffed. "She hates me."

"She's protective," Rikki argued.

I stood. "All right. Let's get this over with."

Chapter Nine

The spectrum of sounds caught me by surprise. Growls, shrieks, groans, and cries overwhelmed the elements of the environment. The pack huddled together on the open patch of grass in the backyard enclosed by trees. My breathing became more ragged, almost as if my lungs had grown to enormous proportions and I couldn't get enough air to fill them completely. Feeling faint, I closed my eyes, but they snapped open a minute later when I felt a vicelike grip on my wrist. It was a member of the pack unknown to me, but her golden eyes indicated that I was about to be introduced to the wolf that lived within her.

I quickly noticed that she was not the only one – each of the pack members were shifting. Skin boiled and ruptured, replaced by thicker tissue and grit. Many of them crouched near to the ground, screaming as each disc of their spines was shattered and remolded. The woman's grip on my wrist tightened. The veins and tendons in my arm were buckling under the pressure. I howled in pain.

Rikki sprinted over to us, removing my wrist from the woman's grasp with ease. I stretched my arm out and shook it violently, trying to relieve myself of the intense pain. There was already some swelling at the site, and I could hardly move it.

"Fuck," I hissed. "I think she fractured my wrist."

Taking my arm in her hands gingerly, Rikki examined the injury. "Yes, she did. But it will heal in a few hours."

I shook my head.

"Please," I pleaded, "tell me about shifting. Will I be in that much pain?"

Rikki nodded somberly. "I will stay by your side."

I wanted to run. I wanted to run far and fast and never turn around to look behind me. I wasn't the cowardly type, but this was not a normal situation. The cells and chromosomes of my form were screaming at me, urging me in two directions – my home and the forest. It was a war between my two natures, and the neophyte wolf was winning by sheer force. I retched chunks of half-digested hamburger that strangled the green of the grass. Rikki's hand slid down my arm and in one smooth movement, she intertwined her fingers with mine. A squeeze. A smile. I took a deep breath.

Rikki surveyed the mass metamorphosis. "It is scary to see the first time."

"I don't think…" I heaved but produced nothing. "Don't leave my side, okay?"

"Promise."

When the transformations were complete, I watched as dozens of wolves of varying size chased each other in an impish manner. They almost seemed friendlier as wolves, reminding me of young children at play. Rikki named each wolf that passed, hoping to help me get accustomed to identifying each member of the pack.

I checked my pulse when I noticed my racing heartbeat. My eyes widened. "My heart's beating 160 a minute!"

"That is normal for a werewolf," Rikki assured me, her hand still holding mine.

My eyes began to water. I panicked. "Is this the start?"

"Take a breath," Rikki cooed, the brown of her eyes melting into gold.

I winced as my skin tightened. I staggered backwards, but Rikki kept my hand in hers. A pounding as heavy and sonorous as a drum erupted from the nothingness in my subconscious. The aching in my gums returned. This was happening. Despite my defiance in the face of Rikki's many warnings. Despite seeing everyone around me turn into wolves. I couldn't think. My skull felt as if it was being crushed repeatedly by some large object. I wrested my hand from Rikki's and pressed both my hands against my head, hoping for some relief.

"Take off your clothes. They will only cause you pain as your body shifts," she instructed.

Under normal circumstances, I would object to removing my clothes in front of a group of strange wolves, but I did as she ordered. I barely finished undressing before pain savaged my collarbone and sternum. I dropped to my knees. I wrapped my arms around my stomach. My ribs were splitting apart. I couldn't breathe. I collapsed on my side. My mind went blank. I dug my fingers into the soil, clawing at the earth in desperation. I screamed. I wanted it to end.

"Fighting it will only make it worse," Rikki counseled, trying to soothe me.

"Please," I begged.

Rikki knelt beside me. "You can do this, Bonnie. Tell your body to shift. Plead for it."

A Night Claimed

I was done. I couldn't struggle against it or the pain anymore. I accepted it. My back arched and a hollow pain tore through my spine. Hair sprouted, claws formed, a snout developed. I disappeared into something new, something that belonged to the forest – the trees, the rivers, the pulsing of blood.

A wolf was born.

*

Cautiously, I opened my eyes. My vision had considerably improved. I spotted a line of ants weaving through clusters of mushrooms at the base of a fir tree. I heard the thumping of a rabbit's hindlegs against the soft earth. The urge to run was consuming. I wobbled, unsteady on my new legs. New instincts and desires flooded my consciousness. I sniffed the air and was bombarded by dozens of scents that battled one another for primacy. I was something else now – a bizarre and elemental being.

Someone brushed against my fur. I looked to my side with my new eyes. It was Rikki. I don't know how I knew it was her, but I did. She was a magnificent wolf. Her black and silver coat was striking in its contrast to the hues of the forest. I wanted to be near her, but I was still shaky in this form. My tail wagged. *I have a tail. This is weird.* Rikki brushed her body against mine again. She was playing with me.

Hesitantly, I took a step. I stumbled like a newborn calf learning to walk for the first time after emerging from the womb. In time, I was brave enough to sprint. I reveled in the caress of the wind against my body, sensing the human Bonnie fade. The wolf was all there was now. The others soon joined, and we cut deep into the woods. Tree limbs stretched low before us, partially blocking our path. The pack dodged each obstacle with ease. Every movement was elegant – muscles worked in tandem with bone.

Chapter Ten

I awoke to a chorus of calm breathing. I rested the weight of my body on my elbows as I lifted my chest and arms off the ground to get a good look at my surroundings. The entire pack was sleeping soundly. The spongy moss underneath my body was cool. *My body.* The fur had vanished and was replaced by the familiar caramel color of my skin. The wolf was gone. I had returned.

I was acutely aware that I was naked. I hastily covered myself with my hands, looking around for anything I could use to help me to feel less exposed. I knew it was silly, especially since the rest of the pack members were naked. I looked around, finding Rosemary near Tato, and Cecilia cuddling with her mate, Toni. It was still dark, but my wolf instinct told me it was early in the morning.

The air was crisp. I wasn't cold, but I wouldn't have refused a blanket at that moment…or clothes. I turned to my side and found Rikki sleeping next to me. Her beauty was wild and dazzling. I slid closer. She was facing me on her side. Her angles were softer somehow. Maybe it was an effect of shifting. I shook my head. I needed to think rationally. But she was mesmerizingly beautiful. I swallowed the lump in my throat.

Damn. Don't fall for her, Bonnie.

Her lips were full and bitable. Rikki's eyes sprang open and I was startled.

"Fuck!" I squealed. "What are you? Lazarus reborn?"

"I was not dead," Rikki quipped.

I narrowed my eyes at her remark.

She grinned. I fell again, spiraling down the tunnel of lust. *Damn.* She had a beautiful smile. I wanted to turn away but knew that was impossible.

"I brought this for you." She offered me a blanket that was stowed beside her on the ground.

"May I?"

I wasn't sure what she was asking permission to do, but I nodded before thinking. Rikki didn't touch me, she merely looked at me, drinking in the view of my body. My nipples hardened. I licked my dry lips, trying to control my breathing. My stomach tightened, and I squeezed my thighs together. I was afraid. If Rikki touched me then I wouldn't have been able to resist her.

"May I?" she asked again.

I should have asked this time what it was she wanted, but I was afraid to. *Coward.* Something inside me sought something from her. I was unsure of what that was, but I knew I would eventually discover it. Some part of me knew it was my newly born wolf driving the desires.

I nodded again. I didn't care if everyone was awake and watching, I couldn't say no to this woman. *Where was the tough, relentless part of me?*

Gentle fingertips lightly grazed my cheek. I shuddered. Rikki's jaw was clenched in restraint. Before Rikki could give in to her yearning, her head abruptly shot up. Her eyes were gold. In one swift motion, she grabbed my arm, pulling me up from the ground. We joined the others who were already awake and golden-eyed. Something was going on.

"Keep her here," Rikki demanded of Rosemary. She then disappeared into the forest.

*

I paced. This is precisely what made me not trust the connection I had with her. I was being foolish thinking this could work. She would always be this dominating ass who lacked the ability to communicate with me properly.

"She's only trying to protect you," Rosemary insisted. She was nervously chewing her fingernails and staring at something past the trees.

"I don't care. I am not a child. And I am not weak!" I bellowed.

"Fuck. Can you calm the hell down? Since you've been here, there has been nothing but anxiety." Cecilia couldn't help herself. She'd never let me forget how much she disliked my presence in the pack.

I glared at her threateningly. I wasn't in the mood tonight. "I will tell you this once, princess! I'm already pissed off at Rikki. Don't make me show you a good ass whooping."

Cecilia rolled her eyes. "I don't see how you're upset with our Alpha. You were just about to—"

"You do know that Rikki can sense Bonnie's tension right now?" Rosemary warned Cecilia.

Rosemary explained to me earlier today that she was a submissive wolf. It was strange. Whenever I saw her at the hospital, she was scary as hell. No one wanted to be on her bad side. Here, she was the exact opposite. I guess humans were submissive to submissive wolves.

I paced for a few more minutes. I reminded myself that I didn't have to follow anyone's orders but my own. I started marching to the house, but Rosemary blocked my path.

"Rikki wants—"

"Rikki should have thought about staying here herself to keep me from leaving!" I was so mad that my heart rate was climbing at an alarming rate. I felt like a caged animal.

"Please, Bonnie." Suddenly, it seemed as if all of Rosemary's energy was sucked out of her, leaving her exhausted. I listened to her this time.

I stared in the direction of the house and then turned back to Rosemary, still feeling conflicted. I was in a whole new world. I knew Rosemary was only trying to keep me safe. It was obvious that Rikki and the others were running toward a threat. I could feel the frenzy sliding up and over me. It was chilling, but that frenzy never overwhelmed me so much that I lost control. I took a deep breath and then another, wanting that cold and feverish sensation to dissolve. I let my rigid shoulders drop.

"Thank you," Rosemary whispered.

"Why are you *thanking* her?" Cecilia shouted. I was starting to think she loved to create drama unnecessarily. "She just did it again! Making us feel what she—"

"Why are you complaining?" It was someone I had not yet met. He crossed his arms over his chest.

Honey-colored eyes reprimanded Cecilia. His blond hair was short, which only drew attention to his slim body. He reminded me of an old friend of mine I had known since middle school. His shoulders were slumped, and there was something about his posture that made me believe he might be a submissive wolf. Far more submissive than Rosemary.

He spoke softly, never raising his voice, "For a few of us who were scared, she helped to calm us. I was ready to shift and hide behind a rock or something."

Cecilia frowned and said nothing. She stormed away from our group.

He looked to be in his mid-20s. Maybe even younger than that, but it was difficult to discern the age of a werewolf.

He smiled at me and I returned his smile. "I'm Greenly."

I shook his hand when he offered it to me. I was relieved to finally meet someone who was kind. I was beginning to think Tato and Rosemary would be all I knew in this…*pack*. That word still was foreign to me.

It took me a little too long to say, "I'm Bonnie."

"And our Alpha's mate. Yes?" someone new interjected.

I could do this. Be friendly. I wouldn't comment on being Rikki's mate yet. It was the last thing I wanted to think about, particularly here, naked in the forest with other naked people. I told myself not to get swept up in the niceties. There was no way I could join their pack. It would be too much for me to handle. But if I didn't join this pack, how could I survive alone?

"So much pressure is on you," Greenly said. "I would not want to be in your shoes."

I bit my lip. "Yes. I'm still in denial, though."

Rosemary hugged me from behind. She rested her head on my shoulder and I leaned against her. What was I doing, letting her or anyone comfort me? That was not something I did. Ever. When I felt tons of emotions piling up on me, I usually hid away from the world, letting it all out privately. I couldn't show my weaknesses in front of all these strangers. In front of Rosemary. In front of Cecilia.

But her touch was intoxicatingly cozy. I could almost fall asleep in her arms. Is this what it felt like to be in a pack? Greenly's hand brushed my other shoulder. His smile was contagious. I smiled in response. My heart fluttered with mixed emotions. I wasn't ready to let them all in. It was a hard thing for me to do.

"Stop fighting us," Rosemary whispered in my ear.

That seemed to do it. Tears burst from my eyes and I shuddered. Rosemary's arms gripped me tighter.

"I thought she was a dominant?" Cecilia asked quizzically. "I mean, Omegas aren't submissive."

Rosemary answered, "Omegas do not merely live as dominant or submissive. She is dominant when she needs to be. Submissive when she needs to be. Only a very few are mostly seen as submissive and Bonnie isn't one of them."

I pulled myself out of Rosemary's arms and wiped my eyes. I reached down to grab a shirt, forgetting that there weren't any clothes out here. The blanket lay several feet behind me on the ground.

"I can—"

I waved dismissively. "No. It's all right."

If everyone else was naked then I really wasn't alone. I smiled awkwardly. There was no hiding my emotions from them.

Everyone's attention was directed toward the house.

"She is calling us to come home," Cecilia announced.

The pack began to walk toward the house. I was about to take a step forward when Rosemary put her hand on my back. "Our Alpha wants you to stay here. She will come to you."

I frowned but nodded. Rosemary flashed me a sympathetic look.

I waited for Rikki alone. She probably knew I was feeling so many conflicting emotions right now and wanted to address them privately. I was not the type of person to air personal grievances publicly. I grabbed the blanket from the ground and wrapped it around myself. I could do this. Face her. I said it over and over again in my head, knowing I had no clue how I would act once I saw her.

*

I was alone. Alone and naked. Alone and naked and Bonnie. My wolf was gone, and so were the others. They had received some telepathic order from Rikki to return to the house. I was to wait here alone. For her. I was still a little fuzzy on the wolf telepathy details, but I knew I would understand it eventually. Hopefully. The birds were announcing the sunrise from their nests, and it was less chilly than earlier. It was peaceful. It was the perfect atmosphere for me to sit in and process my first experience as a wolf. But of course, with my luck it wasn't going to happen.

I sensed something approaching me at a rapid pace. I didn't panic. I knew it was Rikki. Her scent was unmistakable. She was 30 feet out. As she closed the distance between us, the wolf became human. Her angles reemerged. I was beginning to really like those angles.

But something was off. Her expression was grave, her eyes remained gold. I was certain she perceived my frustration at being forced to remain behind by myself. I wasn't accustomed to being ordered about, and even though I understood that she was Alpha and that I would have to get used to the dynamics of the pack, I wasn't quite there yet. I hadn't let go of my autonomy.

I knew she was upset about something, but I needed to tell her that I was upset too.

"Look, I do not appreciate being bossed around, especially when I am new to the circumstances and the people…well, the wolves."

Rikki was silent for a second and then said, "I understand. Accepting this…is not easy, I should know. I didn't ask for this life either, and only in the last several years have I truly embraced this identity."

The smallest breeze could have knocked me flat on my back. Not once did I ever consider how this life might not have been an entirely positive experience for her. I became angry at myself for not making much of an effort to assimilate into the pack. In fact, I did everything I could so far to separate myself from the others. From Rikki. The two of us were more alike than I imagined. I wanted to say something, to apologize, but I was unable to even open my mouth.

Soft hands found my shoulders. I resurfaced into awareness, realizing that it was Rikki's hands on me. I didn't want to push her away. At least, not right now. I needed the comfort that she wanted to provide. She moved closer to me and pressed her forehead against mine. Her warmth entered my body. I closed my eyes.

"Everything I'm doing is for the protection of the pack…and you."

"What were you protecting me from?"

Rikki's body stiffened. "A rogue who claims his Alpha attacked you. They crossed our boundary."

I was instantly alert. "What did they want?"

"To meet. With you there."

"Why would he want me—"

"He made you. He technically has… rights to you."

I scowled and shifted my weight to one leg. "What does that mean? Rights to me? No one has rights to me!"

She didn't say anything.

Terror washed over me. "You would hand me over—"

"Never," Rikki snapped, the gold in her eyes flickered. "But by werewolf law, one who creates a wolf has a claim to that wolf for their pack or mate. Anyone who goes against that law is punished."

"I'm not going with him."

Rikki chuckled. "I figured you'd say something like that."

"So, then what's the plan?"

She chewed on the inside of her lip thoughtfully. "First, let's go back to my house and dress. Then, we'll talk."

*

"Do I scare you?" Rikki looked up at me from her place on the couch.

I was pacing the floor in the living room of her little shed after we finished dressing. Her question irritated me.

"No. Right now, whatever is happening between you and me is the last thing on my mind. I-I just…all I can think about is the wolf that attacked me. He's coming for me. He and his Alpha want to *claim* me."

She waited patiently for me to finish, then said, "We *will* figure this out."

I scratched the back of my head anxiously. "I...I want to go home."

As if in response, the door opened. It was Rosemary.

"Take her home," Rikki said barely above a whisper.

Rosemary never spoke a word. After that exchange I didn't speak either. I could only think of my bed and those yellow eyes. I wondered if the image of those eyes would ever disappear.

Chapter Eleven

On the way back home, I called my supervisor. She wanted me to come into the office. I was nervous and eager all at once. It had been too long since I worked a shift on the rig, and I was desperate to return to the grind. But honestly, at this point I'm sure I would have been happy to get intense dental work done if it took me away from Mill City and anything involving werewolves. I only stayed at my house long enough to shower and change, and I did it all at top speed.

Once at the station, I knocked on the door to my supervisor's office. The main office was a wide square, housing a row of mini offices in an L-shape. The manager was not in today. He was never here on weekends. My supervisor was on the phone. She waved me in. Her desk and office were incredibly organized. She sat behind the desk, a look of exasperation plastered on her face.

I had missed this place sorely. All I wanted was to hop in an ambulance and speed off in any direction. It wasn't only about the thrill or the odd calls that made me love my work. It was about the people who relied on me. It was about knowing that I made a difference. As cliché as it was, I chose this career because I loved helping others. When I was young, I was so wrapped up in my own heartaches, always thinking the worst of the world.

However, since I began this career, things improved dramatically for me. I saw people who struggled or let their weaknesses overpower them. The homeless, the drug addicts, and those having psychiatric emergencies. How could I dwell so heavily on my own life when I saw others at their worst? It was hard. There were days I wanted to quit. But, then where would I be? Who would I be? I was proud to be a paramedic.

Nothing would stop me from returning to work. Not Rikki, Rosemary, or even myself.

She hung up, putting her cell phone on the desk with some force. "Sorry about that. We keep jumping in and out level zero. That was medic seven-two. They had a cardiac arrest call and are now on their way here for more supplies."

I smiled, not sure what to say.

"Follow me." Supervisor Kelly rose from her chair, studying me and seemingly assessing my mobility. "I heard you'd been healing quickly."

"Yeah…" I replied as I followed her.

"How are you feeling?" she asked.

I shrugged, which was a waste of time since her back was turned to me. We went through the door and headed to the ambulance bay. I proceeded behind at a comfortable distance.

"I'm ready to get back to work," I blurted out.

"I'm sure." She laughed and kept walking.

I reminded myself that I had an abnormally fast recovery. If I pushed to get back to work too soon, it might raise questions. I didn't want to have any more attention on me.

"Just missing the job," I added with a nervous chuckle.

We went into the supply room, and I watched as Kelly began gathering extra stock.

"Everyone misses you. Even the fire crews," Kelly joked, moving items from the shelves into a box.

I snorted and began helping her with the inventory. "I bet."

"The reason I called you in today is because I heard what happened at the hospital." She paused, looking to me for a quick answer. After a moment of waiting, she went back to collecting the rest of the supplies for medic seven-two.

My heart sputtered, unsure of what she was referring to and suddenly worried my job was on the line.

"You had a panic attack? Right?"

I clenched my jaw once I remembered that night. I hated that the hospital could be a hotbed of vile gossip at times. The so-called 'panic attack.' It was the night I could not sleep and decided to go to the hospital because I didn't know where else to go. It was also the night I met Rikki.

I clicked my tongue twice. "Not my proudest moment."

"Look…" She abruptly stopped talking when medic seven-two pulled up in front of the garage.

We approached the ambulance as the medics parked.

"Hey, Bonnie! Missing us?" Kenneth teased as the window of the rig rolled down.

"You wish." I rolled my eyes, but I was concerned that he also knew about the hospital incident.

Kenneth was in the driver seat with a new partner at his side. We introduced ourselves and made small talk for a few minutes until a call came through on the radio.

"The life," Kenneth remarked. "All right. It was good seeing you, Bonnie. Get back to work. Stop being lazy!"

The ambulance pulled out of the bay with its lights flashing. I smiled absently, wishing I could be with them in the rig.

"You'll be back soon." Kelly could see the longing in my eyes. "Let's head back to my office."

Once we returned to Kelly's office and we were both seated, she pulled out a folder and held it open to me.

"The manager and all us *sups* want to ensure you make a full recovery. Since you weren't injured while on duty, you aren't eligible for workers' comp, but if you like, we can put you on light work duty. It's not ideal, I know, but it's something to consider." She flipped to the next set of papers. "These papers you will need to fill out to return to duty."

I skimmed the papers. Apparently, I would need to be cleared by a doctor in order to return to work. It was reasonable, but I wondered if they would find anything *abnormal.*

"We would also like you to see a therapist. Your mental well-being is just as important as your physical well-being."

"See a mental health professional?" I asked brusquely. I shouldn't have been as surprised as I was.

Kelly leaned back against her chair. "There's nothing wrong with seeing a therapist. I see one."

"I have a mentor. Can't I just—"

"This is different. This is a personal trauma, and it must be taken seriously."

I sighed, looking down at the papers.

"The sooner you see someone, the sooner you will be cleared."

I knew she was right. Although, what was I supposed to tell a therapist? That I was attacked by a wolf that was actually a werewolf? Now I'm a werewolf too? I would end up in a mental institution.

"Thank you," was all I could manage to say.

Kelly nodded. She laced her fingers together across her stomach. "Continue to heal, and please keep us updated. We all really want you back out there."

"I appreciate that." I stood. "See you soon."

*

I knew trying to get back on duty would upset Rikki. It wasn't the best idea, to be honest. I was new to this supernatural world. *What if I lose control and attack a patient?* I was so confused. I sat in my car in front of my house considering my options. Mindlessly scrolling through the numbers in my phone, I made a decision. I called Rosemary and asked her to meet me for drinks tonight.

For the next couple of hours, I tried to keep myself occupied so I wouldn't think so much about everything that was going on, but I was unsuccessful. Anxiety got the better of me, so I opted to head to the bar where Rosemary and I planned to meet. I was early. It was a casual place. The owners made their affinity for wood painfully clear. Wooden tables. Wooden stools and chairs. Wooden walls and floors. I found a table tucked in the corner of the bar and made myself comfortable.

The bartender approached, smiling widely. Too many teeth showing for my comfort level. At least they were white.

"You're new?" he asked, still smiling.

"Umm." I smacked my lips, trying to come up with something witty to say. "Last I checked, I have been a semi-regular customer of yours, Bill."

He grinned mischievously. "Huh. Well I'll be damned, Bonnie. First round of drinks is on me."

"Can you add two burgers with that?"

"Sure thing. Have to keep that appetite in check." He winked and walked away, returning a moment later with my drink. "Those burgers will be right up."

"Thanks."

The bar door opened, and Rosemary strolled in, immediately spotting me at my table. She did not look happy.

"Something happen?" I asked when she arrived at the table.

"Of all the bars in town you choose this one," she said exasperatedly.

I looked around, curious as to why she seemed so unhappy to be in this bar. "What's wrong with it? I've been coming here for the last two years."

Rosemary scoffed. "Of course you have. Becoming one of us was fate, it seems."

"Hey, hey," I snapped. I wanted her to keep quiet about the wolf thing.

Rosemary gestured around the room. "This is a *werewolf* bar, Bonnie. You've been coming to a werewolf bar for two years!"

"Fuck me," I muttered in disbelief, burying my face in my hands.

"You should really learn how to use your nose. You could have easily caught the scent of werewolves if you tried a little."

"There's a wet dog smell all over this place. How could I pick up the scent of werewolves?"

The looks I got from some of the bar patrons would have terrified Genghis Khan.

"Hey now. She was my favorite human. Give her a break," Bill told the customers. "She doesn't realize that's how she smells now too."

Maybe Rikki was right. She told me the other night that my mouth would get me in trouble. In the human world, I did just fine. But since the moment I was attacked, anything I said seemed to antagonize everyone around me.

"Say *sorry*," Rosemary whispered to me across our small little table.

"Oh." I looked up. "My bad. Sorry."

In the space of a second everyone was relaxed again. No more stiff shoulders or random growls. When I looked at Rosemary, I noticed she was shaking a little. She was in a bar filled with dominant werewolves. I reached over the table and grabbed her hand.

"Sorry," I said it to her this time. "I take it that you don't go out to werewolf bars."

"I do but only with a few dominant wolves in my pack. Not alone."

"We can go," I offered.

Bill returned to the table to deliver the two burgers.

"Welcome to the pack," Bill whispered, leaning across the table so I would hear.

"Pack." I let the word linger on my tongue, trying to embrace it.

"You are the new wolf everyone has been talking about," he continued. "I am one of Rikki's wolves."

"Oh," I replied, failing at being polite. I had no clue how to respond, especially since I still wasn't sure of my own wishes regarding the pack.

He seemed to sense my discomfort and left Rosemary and me alone to talk.

I had already started eating when Rosemary asked, "Why did you want to meet up?"

"Just to talk."

"Bullcrap." Rosemary's brow arched. "What did you do? And is it going to piss off our…" she noticed my frown from her referring to Rikki as *our*, and rephrased, "*my* Alpha?"

I pursed my lips, considering my answer. Technically, I hadn't done anything wrong yet. I wiped my mouth with a napkin and cleared my throat with a gulp of beer. "*Define* actions that would piss her off?"

It was a reasonable question.

Rosemary groaned exaggeratedly. "Bonnie, not one day since your first shift and—"

"I never said I did anything wrong," I clarified. *Wait. Why am I acting concerned about what Rikki would think?* "I'm asking a fair question."

"You should probably just tell me what you did. Tato and a few from our… I mean, *my* pack will be here in the next 10 minutes."

"What?" I snarled.

Rosemary shuddered.

Oops. "Sorry. I was hoping for a one-on-one. I'm not ready for a werewolf group outing."

Rosemary rolled her eyes at my choice of words.

"Fine." I needed to be quick. "My supervisor called me in today. She wants me to make the preparations necessary so that I can return to work."

"Preparations," she repeated.

"What I need to do in order to be cleared to work."

"And you told her that you needed more time than you thought, right?" When I said nothing, Rosemary slammed her drink down. Probably a little harder than she had intended.

"Was I supposed to say that?" I asked.

"Yes," she responded without hesitation.

I frowned. "This is my career! If I told her I needed time off, it would raise questions. They already want me to be cleared by a therapist as well as a doctor. How do you think that makes me feel?"

"And you don't often hear about unsuspecting paramedics being attacked by a werewolf." Rosemary finally took a bite of her burger.

"If werewolves are just walking around us every day, why haven't we questioned others about this rogue pack?"

"That's not something we need to discuss here." Rosemary dropped her burger on her plate.

The bar went silent.

A surly-looking man approached our table. He appeared to be in his early 40s. The light grey in his black hair was striking. His eyes narrowed on me as he rested one of his hands at the back of my chair.

I stared at Rosemary in confusion. "Did I say something wrong?"

"Yes," he growled, instantly catching my attention. "And I advise you to be quiet on the matter you were just discussing."

I arched my brow, turning my gaze to him. Something snapped. "I'm sorry, I was only discussing the situation as to how I became a werewolf. Does my topic bother you because you were involved—"

No other words could escape my mouth. He rammed his fist into my chest in one fluid motion. It felt like being hit by a steam shovel. I wheezed as I flew out of my chair. I collapsed, gasping for air. I twisted to my side. I could barely breathe from the pain.

My vision was blurry, but I could make out Rosemary's form. She was hunched over on her knees in fear. She had begun to shift.

I heard something click. I looked up. It was Bill, and he was pointing a shotgun at the man who assaulted me. "You made a fucking mistake touching her."

"She should learn her place!" the man roared.

The door swung open, and I could hear grumbling and angry words being exchanged. Then, there was nothing. Then, it was all black.

Chapter Twelve

I shuddered, sensing heat on my skin. I shifted my body against soft cushions. A powerful wave of nausea contorted my stomach into iron knots. I wanted to vomit but that would require me to move, and that was not going to happen. I would have rather aspirated on my vomit.

I heard light but determined footsteps. A chair slid across the floor.

"Can you open your eyes?"

I squeezed my eyes shut tightly in protest for exactly eight seconds before trying to open them. The light in the room was miserably bright.

"Where am I?" My voice sounded gravelly.

I blinked rapidly, taking a moment to adjust to the brightness in the room. I was in Rikki's shed. My chest hurt, but my collarbone was no longer broken. All that was left was some bad bruising and pain.

"How long have I been out?"

"Several hours." Rikki was leaning forward in her chair, her hands in her lap.

One of her legs was shaking erratically. Rage emanated from her like heat from a campfire.

I sat up slowly and not without difficulty. I was on her couch. *What could I say? I'd rather not have her blow up at me.*

"I'll leave." I moved to the edge of the couch, endeavoring to put distance between us.

"Sit. Back. Down." Every word was slow and terrifying.

"I'm really not in the mood for this."

"Now, Bonnie." Her eyes were gold when they met mine. She was gnashing at her inner bottom lip. She took a deep breath. "How do you feel?"

"I'm fine, *mother*." I made no attempt to hide my sarcasm.

"You think what happened is a joke? Do you know what could have happened?"

"What are you talking about?"

"Challenging an unknown werewolf is dangerous even on the best of days but challenging one when you are a newborn wolf is just plain moronic." She stood abruptly, and in the blink of an eye she sped from her chair to the fireplace that was four feet away. "You risked your life. Rosemary's life!"

"I didn't do anything wrong." I scowled in defiance. "I never threatened—"

"Mockery. Rude remarks. Sarcasm. You were basically telling that werewolf that you didn't take him seriously. That he is unimportant. That you are not concerned about what he can do to you."

"I wasn't." I pressed my hand against the pain in my ribcage. "He butted into my conversation. He had no right—"

"Perhaps not." Rikki's eyes narrowed again as she interrupted me once more. She returned to her chair in front of me. "You can't continue to speak to others as you do to humans. You are no longer a human. And to a werewolf...if you use sarcasm or any form that can be a means to challenge them, they have a right to prove they are the stronger werewolf. Living as dominant wolves, that means something. For you…an Omega…your life is doubly at risk. You are not capable of submitting unless you truly choose. And to werewolves that is another slap in their faces."

I shook my head. "I didn't ask for this. Fuck this. Fuck you and your fucking…crazy ass rules!" I waved my hands frantically. "I am not a freaking coward and I will not let anyone come at me the way he did. Fuck that."

"Then you will die." Both her tone and expression were grave. Sincere.

"Perhaps I should have died when I was attacked."

I knew it was anger and grief speaking. Why was I feeling so overwhelmed with emotions?

"I can't. I will not be belittled. Degraded. For anyone. Never. It is not in my nature to bow." I wiped my tears as they fell. The frustration of this conversation broke my emotional barrier into tiny fragments.

"I am not asking you to submit to any man or woman who offends you." Her look told me she had a *but* coming. "Yet, you are in a new world. You will die within the first year if you don't understand…there is a new language you must learn. And in that, you will learn how to defend yourself from those who challenge, question, or offend you without starting a fight. You cannot avoid this."

"I just don't see how this is my fault. I didn't want to fight—"

"I know you didn't. But now…in this new world you live in, what you say, more importantly, *how* you speak matters. Rosemary is a submissive wolf. She was so terrified by what happened that it took me an hour to get her out from underneath the table."

My eyes widened when I realized how stupid I had been acting. This was no longer about me anymore. I *was* in a whole new world whether I accepted it or not. The last thing I wanted was to die over dumb words. Dumb choices. And Rosemary. My ignorance put her in danger.

"I wanted to kill him for touching you. Tato was wise to send him off. But I think…you wouldn't want me playing hero for you. You are clearly not weak. And…I think it is time to teach you how to speak our language. How to fight our way. So that when the time comes, you'll know how to protect yourself."

I was exhausted, exasperated, and in pain. She was right. "How is Rosemary?"

Rikki smiled. "She is well. Concerned for you."

I nodded. I was still acting like my life never changed. I needed to learn and adjust.

"I'm sorry."

Rikki reached out her hand to brush my cheek. "You are learning. And it means a lot to Rosemary and me that you are willing to try."

I leaned into her palm. The warmth of her hand brought me comfort.

"And to be clear, we *are* still investigating the rogue. I should have kept you informed."

"I want to be involved."

"Bonnie." Rikki sighed heavily.

"I want to be involved. Do whatever you must. Teach me how to be a werewolf. Teach me how to defend myself and let me help. I can't sit on the sidelines. That rogue destroyed my human life."

Rikki lowered her head in acceptance.

I smiled weakly in relief. I needed her support. "I should…go talk to Rosemary."

*

I found Rosemary sitting on the couch in the main house. Tato sat beside her, speaking softly in her ear. When they noticed me, Tato got up and gestured for me to sit in his place. I did so without hesitation.

"So, I guess I fucked up."

"You didn't know any better, Bonnie. I am not—"

"Please, don't make excuses for me. It's too late. Rikki has already made me feel extremely guilty. I was reckless. Stupid."

Rosemary fiddled with the buttons on her shirt. "I appreciate you saying that."

"I mean it."

"I know you do." Rosemary shoved my shoulder playfully. "Stop looking so defeated. I'm okay."

I patted her leg.

"Have you at least told Rikki about you returning to work?"

Well, so much for a pleasant conversation.

"Nope. Being knocked unconscious for a while pretty much delayed that particular discussion."

"The longer you wait—"

"Are you planning to tell her?" I asked.

"*You* should tell her," Rosemary urged.

"That wasn't a *no*."

"She's my Alpha. If she asks me, I have to tell her the truth."

I scowled. "Fuck, Rosemary! I respect how you feel about the pack laws, but this is my life. My choices."

Rosemary stared at her feet. "I get it. All I'm saying is that until you know what you can handle, perhaps you should lean on me or Rikki. We are both here for you."

Rosemary gave me a cheeky smile as I headed for the front door after we shared an embrace. Ready to face the Rikki roller-coaster, I grumbled and made my way back to her shed.

As soon as I opened the door, I realized I should have knocked first. I heard Celtic music playing in the background. Rikki wasn't in sight. Closing the door, I called out in a small voice, suddenly feeling like a creeper sneaking in.

"What am I doing?" I mumbled to myself.

I turned to leave and then a door opened. One I hadn't seen before. It was on the other side of the shed next to the kitchen.

Rikki emerged, naked and wet.

Silence. Not even a fucking cricket.

Damn.

"Bonnie." My name being called shook me out of a trance.

I looked up to meet her eyes.

"I...oh..." I swallowed. "I came..."

I had to really think about why I came. *Gosh. Snap out of it, Bonnie.*

Rikki waited. Staring. Naked and wet.

I shook my head and put my hand over my eyes. "Can you like...put on clothes?"

"This is my space," Rikki said.

As she went to her room and dressed, I explained, "I should have knocked. This is your space and—" I stopped myself and frowned. "Wait...you knew I'd be coming back, right?"

"I can't read your mind, Bonnie. If I could, I would have avoided you stabbing me with a pen."

I ignored that.

"No," I retorted. "You are a werewolf. You had to smell me coming. Or Rosemary sent you some magic signal. You did this on purpose. You wanted me to catch you…like this."

Rikki laughed. "Then explain to me…how was I to know you'd just barge into my shed? Maybe I thought you'd knock."

She had a point there. *Son of a bitch. How could I counter that?*

"Bonnie, the last thing I want is to seduce you into my bed…only for you to regret it later. Like you said, whatever is happening between us is the last thing on your mind. We will have our time."

Now that she was dressed, she sauntered past me to the kitchen.

"You should eat."

"Is that an order?"

"Why do you take everything I say the wrong way?"

"Because you make it so easy." I smiled, enjoying the playfulness of our conversation.

There was something about her that made me feel relaxed. I was reluctant to let go of that feeling.

"I should go. I will grab something to eat on my way home."

Rikki nodded.

I was about to leave but turned back to face Rikki. I reminded myself of why I came back to her shed. "I know the big issue has been me learning to trust you, but I ask you trust me too. There is something I'm not telling you, but…I just…I want to figure it out on my own."

Rikki looked as if she wanted to say something, but she didn't.

"I promise to talk to you about it once I sort it all out in my own head."

"Fair enough."

That was it? No argument? I smiled, relieved and partly disappointed. I couldn't help but enjoy our quarrels. "Okay then."

I clapped my hands together, signaling the end of the conversation.

Rikki was smiling at my sluggish exit. "You sure you want to leave?"

I rolled my eyes. "I was only going to give you an invite. My roommates are throwing me a 'you're still alive celebration.' Since you like parties..." I was referring to the gatherings Rikki created with her pack. I knew a pack gathering and party was two different things. "I wanted to invite you. And Rosemary, of course. Even Tato. I don't know much about the others."

I meant her entire pack. The last thing I wanted was to invite every werewolf in Mill City.

"Are you asking me because you want me there or are you afraid I'll just crash it anyway?"

"Both. But, more than anything...I would like you to be there. So please come."

Rikki arched both brows in amusement.

I smiled. "Just be there."

I walked out with Rikki still giggling behind me.

Chapter Thirteen

I could hear people trickling into my house. I was hiding out in my room. I didn't know how to face anyone yet, especially those friends and my family that I'd been neglecting since my attack. I regretted agreeing to this night. Lying to everyone was the last thing I wanted to do, but I couldn't tell the truth. The party that Sandy and Alicia organized for my recovery seemed like it was in full-swing. I knew I should be out there enjoying it too.

I must have grabbed the doorknob at least ten times, believing I was ready to greet everyone. *So naïve.* I counted to three on the eleventh attempt, and then opened the door to a barrage of various scents which invaded my nostrils. I had to wipe my watering eyes. Perfumes, food, and human sweat. The scent of old blood. It was probably lingering on one of my coworkers from an earlier shift on the rig.

"Oh, there she is!" Jr. cheered.

A few turned to acknowledge me, wide smiles adorning their faces. A few hugged me.

"You look good," Sandy remarked.

I smiled politely. "Thanks. I feel good."

As soon the focus was no longer on me, and I finally relaxed. I think I managed to eat about three hamburgers before Alicia surprised me with a tight embrace from behind.

My entire body froze. My eyes burned and my gums ached.

"What's up with your eyes?" Jr. asked, bewildered.

"Yeah. They are gold," Sandy noted.

"Are you wearing contacts or something?" Jr. asked.

"Is that even a thing?" Alicia wondered aloud.

I could not speak. I could feel my teeth changing and if I opened my mouth, they all would see. I shut my eyes and turned away from my friends, deciding to head to the kitchen to calm down. Being grabbed from behind triggered something inside me. My hands shook and images of torn flesh flashed through my mind.

I balled my hands into fists and slammed them against the countertop.

"You okay, honey?" It was my mother.

She grabbed my arm and I snarled, yanking my arm free of her grip.

Everything was quiet. *What the hell am I doing here?* Rosemary warned me. Rikki warned me. All I wanted was one fucking normal night.

"Did you take your pain meds?" *Rosemary.* She held me firmly.

I knew she was saying that for the benefit of anyone within earshot who didn't know I was a werewolf.

I shook my head.

"How about I help you to your room? I'll give you your meds, we will splash some cool water on your face, and you'll come back out looking brand new," Rosemary offered, continuing to speak loudly.

I only nodded. I walked to my room with Rosemary's assistance. She shut the door behind us. Rikki was already inside waiting with a plate of steak in her hand.

"Eat. And don't argue." Rikki held the plate out for me.

I listened.

After finishing a pound of rare steak, I sat on my bed calmly.

Rosemary stood. "I will give you two a moment and let everyone out there know you are okay."

"Thanks."

Once the door was closed, Rikki came to my side, lifting my chin up to meet her eyes. "You scared me."

"I scared myself," I admitted.

Her hand was soft on my skin. Listening to my own heartbeat, I relaxed knowing that I wanted to be honest with her.

"I was afraid," I said, my hands resting in my lap. "I thought…I was going to do something I couldn't take back. I am really glad you came."

"I promised." Her smile was infectious. Her eyes softened.

My heart was sputtering. It was difficult for me to resist Rikki's comforting arms. I leaned into her embrace. I never thought I would need others this much. Rikki was right about werewolves needing to be touched. This was another strange and new sensation in this strange and new world I now belonged to.

The door to my room opened. My mother walked in from the hallway. I looked from over Rikki's shoulder and observed my mom's lips pursed in an inquisitive expression.

"Um, honey? We, uh, we're waiting on you." She left as quickly as she had arrived.

"Shit," I muttered. "Why didn't you tell me—"

Rikki laughed as I shoved her away, flustered by her nearness. "You have a nose of your own. Use it."

"Whatever." I ignored Rikki's grin. She was laughing at me. "You know what's going to happen now, right?"

"What's that?"

"My mom's going to think we're together now."

Rikki straightened her shirt as she rose from her place on the bed. "Bonnie, it was just a hug."

I rolled my eyes. "Let's go."

*

The party continued without a hitch. At nearly midnight, most left except for a few stragglers. Rosemary approached me when Rikki needed to make a phone call.

"You two look cozied up," Rosemary pointed out.

I snorted. "I'm sure that pleases you."

"Only if you don't take it all back later," Rosemary said. "I know there's a lot you have to work on, but I hope you can at least get to know her and our pack."

"I enjoy our back and forth bantering, though," I joked.

I spied my mom staring at me from the living room. My brothers had left with the first wave of guests some time ago. I waved Rosemary off and headed to the living room where my mom was sitting on the couch.

"Hey, mom." I smiled sheepishly.

She studied me for a minute and then her attention was drawn to what was left of the crowd in the house. "You have supportive friends."

"Yeah."

She found Rikki amidst everyone and frowned. She still wouldn't look at me. "You've always told me about your love life. You are not one to keep secrets from me, Bonnie."

I lowered my head and started fidgeting with the belt loops of my pants. "I know, mom."

"Then why?"

What was I supposed to say? I was attacked by a werewolf and not a wolf? I was no longer human? I was beginning to like a woman who was from a world that was anything but mundane? I couldn't say anything like that. It was true that Rikki and I had a strong attraction to one another despite how I acted toward her, but I was in no shape to entertain that possibility right now. Although, I didn't want to pretend as if there wasn't anything between us at all.

"At least tell me about her?" She finally looked at me. Her gaze was piercing, searching for some truth only I could provide.

I raised my head slightly, and my fingers found employment with the bottom button of my shirt.

"She's..." I stopped and reconsidered my answer. I had to be cautious. "Rosemary was my nurse when I was attacked. Well, we've known each other through work for a few years."

She popped the knuckles of her left hand. She remained seated. Staring. "I know Rosemary. She took great care of you and told us how she enjoyed working with you when you brought patients into the hospital."

I knew she wasn't looking for information regarding Rosemary.

I took a deep breath. "Yeah. We became close friends during my stay in the hospital. She thought I needed some therapy to help me cope with the trauma of the attack. That's how I met Rikki."

I had her complete attention at the mention of Rikki's name.

"Rikki owns some land in Mill City and sometimes, she invites me out there to stay and escape for a bit. It's peaceful out there."

"And she...?" My mom flicked her wrist forward, urging me to continue.

I licked my lips, suddenly feeling more nervous than I thought I could be in this situation. "She's a friend, mom. Right now, she is just a friend."

"Well, all right." My mom gave me a knowing smile.

She couldn't keep her eyes away from Rikki for very long. I was certain that my mother could sense my feelings for Rikki. She was an incredibly perceptive person. I only hoped that she would drop the subject for now since I still wasn't sure of my own feelings. I also was certain that Rikki heard everything I'd said to my mom.

"I only want happiness for you, Bonnie. You know that."

"I know, mom." I leaned in and kissed her cheek.

Rikki took the initiative to come and introduce herself to my mom. That caught me by surprise, but I wasn't against the idea. They exchanged small talk for a while before my mom was ready to leave.

*

I was saying my goodbyes and feeling ready to collapse onto my bed when Rikki suddenly stiffened.

My brows knitted quizzically. "What's wrong?"

"Uninvited guest," Rikki mumbled angrily.

Rosemary shifted her weight on her legs nervously. "What do we do?"

"Just keep yourself in control."

"Stay close to me," Rikki ordered.

The doorbell rang.

Rikki opened the door to reveal an incredibly masculine man. Seriously masculine. His smile was haunting. His power was palpable. Familiar. We were linked. Soil and roots. Moon and tides. I let my eyes linger on him for a time, trying to think of where I'd seen him before. My flesh tingled, and I knew there was something threatening about his presence. He smiled at me, but there was something in his eyes that made me want to flee.

His brown eyes were fixed on mine. "I am so glad to see that you are all right."

He took a step into the house and coldness flooded me like an icy river.

"I am the man who saved you."

That was the last thing I expected to hear. I always wondered about the man who had rescued me from certain death the night I was attacked, but it couldn't be this man standing in front of me now. The aura around him was unsettling and savage, but I was drawn to him like a magnet. *No, it can't be him.*

"Oh, my God! Yes!" Alicia clapped her hands together. "We met you the night of her attack. He stayed with you until we came."

I glared at Alicia, stunned that she never mentioned him being at the hospital. "This is really him?"

"Yes!" Sandy replied excitedly. "I invited him here tonight. I thought you'd want to meet him."

He ignored the gaze of everyone else in the room. There was only him and me for a time. The others slipped away into the background, almost as if they were simply extra decorations for the party. Didn't matter. As much as I wanted to hide from him, I wouldn't let him intimidate me.

"Perhaps we should postpone this. I can see my presence is upsetting." He smiled coolly, his head tilted slightly to the side. "Until next time."

He turned around and disappeared into the night air without another word. Alicia and Sandy were speechless as they stared at the doorway where he had been only seconds before. Rikki shut the door without hesitation, probably wanting to rid the room of his memory.

"Make sure he leaves," she barked at Tato through gritted teeth.

I was thankful that he was gone and that I had been gifted this evening to make up for lost time. I hadn't realized until now that I was neglecting so many of the people who been there for me long before Rikki and the new world.

Rikki and Rosemary followed me to my room.

"I guess I'll pack my bag," I declared without any measure of excitement.

"You are going to come with us tonight? Willingly?" Rikki's eyes widened in genuine surprise.

"Were you planning to let me stay here?"

Rikki clicked her tongue. "Of course not."

"There you go." I pulled out a small duffel bag from underneath the bed. "No sense in arguing with you."

I tried to hide my shaking hands as I dug through my drawer for clean clothes. I was too much of a coward at the moment to tell Rikki I was scared to stay here tonight.

That werewolf might come back. I wasn't sure what would happen if he did.

If Rikki knew I was lying about my reasons for cooperating, she didn't say anything. I was unable to meet her eyes while I continued packing.

"You can trust me and my pack," Rikki assured me encouragingly.

"We want you safe," Rosemary echoed.

It didn't make me happy to realize that I had to rely on others to keep me safe. I'd been independent for so long, and I was reluctant to release the reins. This was new. Being vulnerable. I didn't want to be taken advantage of or thought of as a weak person. But here in this moment, Rosemary and Rikki were telling me that they wouldn't abuse my trust or take my independence from me. That was such a relief.

But I couldn't help myself when it came to thinking about the man who had strolled into the house tonight. My instincts were calling out to me, warning me that this was the man who had turned me. I knew it.

Soil and roots. Moon and tides.

Chapter Fourteen

"You can stay in the main house. There's always a few wolves around."

Rikki was working hard to keep me calm. She had been talking nonstop since we left my house. Long drive. The main house loomed menacingly in my view. I didn't want to stay at the pack's house, but Rikki insisted. I really wasn't in a position to argue. She swore it was temporary. I could only hope that was true.

It was the middle of the night. The house was eerily silent.

Rosemary emerged in the doorway at the front of the house.

"Let her take you to your room," Rikki implored.

I pressed the palm of my hand against my forehead. "Um, yeah. Thanks for letting me crash here, *temporarily.*"

Rikki flashed me an amused smile.

I threw my duffel bag over my shoulder as I climbed out of the car. Rosemary seized it from me the moment my shoes touched the dark wood of the porch. She didn't say a word. We navigated the hallways and then the stairway in silence. Up until this point, I'd never been upstairs. The upper floor was U-shaped, with six bedrooms and two baths. Rosemary led me to the room at the end of the hallway.

A Night Claimed

The room was bigger than I expected. It was bathed in hues of green and gold with Mediterranean décor. Two thick, glass doors rose from the floor nearly to the ceiling on the back wall and opened to reveal a stone balcony. I stepped onto it and the smell of wet earth welcomed me. It was difficult to see anything other than the black sky and the dense forest of trees, but I was able to make out the edges of Rikki's shed poking through the overgrowth. I wondered if she was there.

Part of me wished she'd invited me to stay in her shed with her. I still wasn't entirely accepted as a member of the pack by the others, and I still couldn't blame them. I hadn't fully accepted myself either.

"This was once Rikki's room." Rosemary's comment reminded me of her presence.

I left the balcony reluctantly, shutting the doors behind me. "Is it okay with the others that I take over Rikki's old room?"

"They understand. This room is in sight of the shed and is strategically in the center of the hallway, so you'll be surrounded by wolves at all times."

Awesome.

"Bathroom is over there." Rosemary pointed to an open door a few feet away from the balcony.

Okay, I can work with that. I definitely didn't want to share a bathroom with dozens of other wolves.

Rosemary was inching toward the bedroom door. "Well, get some rest. I'll see you in the morning."

As soon as I heard the *click* of the door, I turned off the light and collapsed onto the bed. I watched the shadows transform and march across the ceiling. Time was going forward, and I was stagnant. Stuck. Stuck to the comforter in defiance, willing myself not to fall into

116

Time's currents. I knew what awaited me. *Who. The wolf.* Soil and roots. Moon and tides. I felt his presence as keenly as I felt air filling and leaving my lungs.

I left the bed and returned to the balcony. Wet earth. I spied Rikki outside, sitting barefoot in the small clearing between the main house and the shed.

Suddenly, I was outside and approaching her, forgetting sleep and promising myself that I'd unpack some other time. Rikki's fingers were burrowing into the dirt.

I cleared my throat. I didn't want to surprise her.

Nothing. The wind whipped through tree branches. I knelt beside her, my chest so low it nearly touched my knees. I tilted my head to get a better look at her face. Rikki's eyes were gold, vibrant, vacant. I sat up and reached my hand out, lightly grazing her shoulder with my fingertips. Her skin was hot. Her head snapped in my direction. Her eyes softened. The gold was gone.

Our foreheads met. Eyes closed. I could hear the steady rhythm of Rikki's breathing. The smell of wet earth mixed with the honeysuckle scent of her skin. My fingers rushed to tangle themselves in her hair. My entire body was humming with expectation. There was no need to use words. Nothing we needed to define now. Just us and the moon. Her lips found mine in the dark, and I was lost to the electric sensation of her kiss.

*

The soft sunlight punched holes in the emerald canopy of the forest. I opened my eyes slowly, letting the yellow rays mold fuzzy forms into focus. Underneath my cheek, the expanding and deflating of Rikki's lungs was conducted at a steady pace. We'd fallen asleep outside. The soil beneath us was dry. I touched my lips lightly, dragging my fingertips along my bottom lip. The electricity was still there, lurking in the memory of the kiss. My stomach growled noisily. Rikki's eyes shot open.

I felt extremely lightheaded. Hunger. The worst kind of pain. I felt as if I hadn't eaten in almost two weeks. I rolled to my side, heaving from nausea. My head hurt. A loud ringing in my ears made me moan. I could barely hear myself.

My muscles were stiff. I could smell everything. Feel everything.

Rikki was standing close to me. I could sense her. Pain shot through my back. I screamed as I felt my ribs stretch and splinter. *What is happening?* I was disappearing. Deeper and deeper into darkness until I was gone.

*

I awoke to find myself naked and covered in dirt. I sat up, scared and unsure of what had happened. All I remembered was pain and hunger.

"I should have made sure you ate something before bed." It was Rikki's voice. She was naked too, standing a few feet from me. She was leaning against a tree.

"I ate." I frowned. "And I knew I was still hungry. I should have gotten something to eat."

"But you didn't—"

"Rikki, I'm an adult. I was hungry, and I ignored it. So, my fault."

She was quiet then. *Good.*

"I shifted, didn't I?"

Rikki smiled. "Oh yeah. And got pretty upset when I tried to hunt for you."

"Hunt?" The thought of killing an animal should have grossed me out, but it didn't. I was merely curious about what happened while the wolf had control. "Hm. Well, that should tell you something. Even as a wolf I don't bow to your every whim."

Rikki shifted against the tree. "Clearly. I bet you are proud of that fact."

"Very."

Without warning, Rikki sped off toward the house. I followed after her, but I was no match for her velocity. At least, not yet. Rikki was already on the porch when I caught up to her. Anxiety saturated my nervous system. We walked through the front door together.

"Please, Alpha," a strange man sobbed as he approached Rikki.

Rikki was kneeling over a motionless body in the living room.

"Isn't there something we can do?" the man wailed, grabbing at Rikki's arms in desperation. "Please!"

A scream, sharp and guttural exploded from the catatonic body. It was a woman. Rikki put her ear against the belly of the woman on the floor, listening intently for any threat.

I took a step forward.

"Stay out of it," Cecilia barked as she blocked my path.

I reminded myself of the conversation I had with Rikki and opted against confrontation. Like it or not, I was in their territory. I sucked on my bottom lip for a minute, then let it go.

"I only want to help. I'm a paramedic."

Cecilia studied me for a moment and then sighed, stepping aside to allow me access to the scene. The closer I came to the trio on the ground, the clearer the situation became – the woman's belly was heavily swollen with child.

"You should have told me your wife was pregnant," Rikki snapped at the man.

He was so preoccupied with his mournful blubbering that he didn't hear her.

She repeated her angry accusation.

He lowered his head in shame. "You've forbidden pregnancy, we know. But we…we always wanted kids."

No children? Why?

"That law was enacted for a reason." Rikki spied my confused expression. "If a female werewolf gets pregnant, the fetus dies upon the first full moon. We are forced to shift, and the transition is too much stress for an unborn child. This is different. She's human. Neither can survive. The two are incompatible."

"So, the baby is doing what specifically?" I asked, sensing the urgency of the situation.

"Trying to rip its way out," Rikki replied, her head still pressed against the woman's stomach.

That was a horror show I did not care to watch.

"I'm sorry," he cried into the woman's ear. He kissed her cheek.

She squirmed and screamed, her fingers drilling into the carpet fibers. I wanted to help. I was a paramedic. I should have been able to. But this was a wolf fetus in a human.

The woman screamed again.

"Can you help me?" Rosemary's question was directed at me. She was carrying an I.V. set.

I nodded hurriedly. I spiked the bag while Rosemary calculated the doses. I realized the medicine they were planning to give her would only help to relieve her pain.

She was going to die.

"What do you think?" she asked me.

I checked the dose. "That's right."

"You want to—"

I shook my head. Under normal circumstances I would start the I.V., but these were not normal circumstances.

Rosemary quickened her pace. Blood sprouted from the flesh where the needle entered. I held my breath, afraid the smell would nudge me into a frenzy. Unfriendly eyes scrutinized my movements.

"I am going to give—"

"No." The words had left my mouth before I even realized it.

Rosemary stared at me blankly.

I moved instinctively. Rikki and Rosemary shuffled backwards, giving me room to work. I pressed my hand down on the firm flesh of her belly. The wolf child countered as I pressed, wriggling in its spongy home. A link formed between us – I could sense a longing to escape the womb, to stretch limbs as far as they could reach. I sat in stunned silence for a moment. *Is that the baby I'm sensing? Its emotions?*

Jesus. How can I be calm now?

I gulped when a wave of nausea threatened a gagging fit. I knew I had to keep it together. I took a deep breath.

"The baby is quite eager to be born." I gave my best reassuring smile to the couple.

The man eyes widened. "You can sense the baby?"

I felt the untrusting gaze of several wolves narrow on me. *Uh-oh.*

"I can hear her...can't you all? Isn't that a werewolf thing?" I glanced from one wolf to another, certain that one of them would confirm my assumption.

"Only between a mated pair, and between an Alpha and their pack. Between any other wolves is extremely rare," Rikki stressed.

"What is she saying?" the woman managed to ask between her cries.

Rikki nodded for me to continue.

"I think she's at full term," I announced aloud.

"Yes. We know this. But a human body won't respond well to giving birth at five or even six months." Rikki furrowed her brows at my assessment.

I closed my eyes, my mind searching for the baby's consciousness.

I smiled after a few minutes.

"What?" the man questioned anxiously.

"The baby will wait."

The woman sat up, no longer feeling discomfort. She took in a few deep breaths. "Thank you."

She hugged me tightly.

"Oh my God, Bonnie!" Rosemary exclaimed. I couldn't tell whether she was happy or horrified. I hoped it was the former.

"Come with me." Rikki left the room, expecting me to follow.

I did. I knew I had to.

When I realized she was leading me to her shed, my shoulders sank. *This isn't going to be good.*

Once we were inside her little home, I spoke first, saying, "Whatever I did in there, I'm sorry."

Rikki planted herself near the fireplace, her shoulder forced against the wall.

"It is rare. No – unheard of, to find a werewolf that was born."

I didn't seek to slow my descent onto the couch. I plummeted at top speed. Thoroughly exhausted. Not at all ready for whatever it was Rikki had to say.

"When I was turned, I had no one. I was orphaned. My mother died of syphilis when I was 12. My father…was Native American. He was killed by the Englishmen for 'seducing' my mother. Being a mixed-race child, I was not allowed to know anything of werewolf history or secrets. I never understood how a werewolf could carry a child to term. Then came the whispers of the Omegas in every Native American pack. They were hidden. Kept safe. Over time, Omegas were hunted or enslaved. Too many Englishmen were being turned into werewolves from random attacks. Native werewolves were being challenged and forced out of their rituals and beliefs."

I couldn't speak. I listened.

"I am sure there are other Omegas out there, but you won't hear talk of them."

"Why are you telling me this now?" I'd been wanting to understand what this all meant for me. Rikki never seemed ready to talk about it before.

Rikki rubbed her chin thoughtfully. "Because, you have done something impossible today. A born werewolf… Tato and I are the only ones who have come across a born werewolf in our long lives. And this is my pack's first time encountering an Omega. This could change the future of our pack, of our species, for the better."

I rested my head against the couch and stared at the ceiling in disbelief.

"Every choice you make is your own. But I'm telling you, we will protect you. Now, more than ever, you need protection. If the wrong people or the wrong *wolves* found out…"

"I really don't have a choice, do I?"

She shook her head slowly. "We are your best chance for some measure of freedom…for life."

There was no other option then. I rubbed my eyes frustratedly, upset in the knowledge that I was going to have to postpone returning to work. Rikki would only say that it was too dangerous, for me and for others. Hell, she didn't even need to say it.

"Okay. Give me some time to digest this. Also, I want to hear from the pack. You know, whether or not they want me to join. I don't want anyone feeling as if they *have* to accept me because of you."

Rikki clenched her jaw. "Fair enough."

*

Everyone was impatiently awaiting our arrival in the main house. Our appearance drew every uneasy gaze. I straightened my back inadvertently. Swallowing the hard lump in my throat, I reminded myself that the pack and me needed each other. The best way for mutual survival. I spotted Rosemary in the crowd. She was clinging to Tato. His arm cradled her waist protectively. Nervous energy buzzed in the air.

Rikki saw no need for procrastination. "I know many of you have questions and serious concerns. To those of you who are familiar with the stories of Omegas and born werewolves, they have always been just that – stories. Whispers of Bonnie had only been just that, whispers. Until she proved otherwise today. I realize that to encounter both of these in the same day must be startling, but we have some decisions to make, and unfortunately, I cannot afford you the time to think on your answers. We need them today. Now."

A man who was introduced to me as Lloyd stepped forward. "I really don't know how I feel about the baby, but I can tell you that this new wolf...*Bonnie*...well, her presence is dangerous. Omegas were hunted for centuries. I-I'm not ready to die for a wolf I don't know."

"The fact that Bonne is an Omega cannot leave this pack, regardless of whether or not she joins. Her connections to us have already been made public, which means that if she is discovered, all wolves will automatically assume she is with us and we will not be safe."

Rikki wasn't giving anyone much of an option.

Cecilia was the next to come forward. "This is a lot to process at once, and I can't help but echo Lloyd's concerns. Despite the miracle she performed today...and I need to say that we are truly grateful for it...despite that, I fail to see how we are supposed to weigh the lives of everyone in the pack against one life. Her life."

Lloyd was right. So was Cecilia. She made a point that no one could ignore. It was plain to see that the others either felt exactly the same way or had similar worries. I didn't want Rikki to speak in my defense. I needed to speak for myself.

I met the gaze of as many of the pack as I could manage. "Look, I understand that I have not made the best impression so far. I've been willful, rude, and I haven't given any of you a reason to *like* me, much less *trust* me. And with this...O-*Omega* business, I wouldn't blame you if you asked me to leave immediately and not come back. But I am here now. I'm willing to learn what it means to be a werewolf. Part of a pack. So, if you can give me a chance to be part of *this* pack, I will embrace it."

Lloyd shifted his weight. He scratched his beard in frustration. "We aren't really considering this, are we? She is our death sentence. For fuck's sake!"

I'd never seen Rikki move that fast before. She was a blur. He was several feet away and she was at his side in less than three seconds. Hands firmly around his throat, Rikki forced Lloyd to his knees. The room was heavy with silence.

"I have been patient with you. You were given the freedom to speak. Not many Alphas would be gracious enough to allow you to be so open." Rikki's voice was gravelly with rage.

Rikki shoved Lloyd on his ass.

She returned her attention to the rest of the pack. "We will vote. Majority rules. Does that seem fair to everyone?"

"Yes, Alpha," a wolf who was Cecilia's mate, Toni replied first. He looked to me. "I vote to accept Bonnie into our pack. We will be stronger together rather than apart."

Cecilia was next. "Yes, Alpha. I vote to accept her into our pack."

That surprised me.

Then Rosemary followed, then Tato, then sweet Greenly, and then many others. Some dissented, but I wasn't angry. We all knew the dangers. There was no turning back now.

"Then it is done," Rikki declared. She took my hand and squeezed.

I smiled. Hopefully convincingly. "Awesome."

Rosemary laughed. "It's all right to be a little freaked out. We all are right now."

"Good, 'cause I'm about ready to pee myself." My joking attitude seemed to ease the tension. *Hopefully.*

Rikki hadn't let go of my hand. "Next full moon we will perform the pack ritual and it will be official."

"What about that rogue bastard?" someone asked.

The air of harmony was fractured.

Well, that didn't last long.

"I think that we need to rest and regroup before we tackle that issue." Rikki nodded her head once and everyone dropped their gaze in response. "Let's meet back here later tonight."

Rikki let go of my hand and walked over to the expecting couple.

"She's going to have them stay here. It will be much safer, and we can monitor the baby's progress." Rosemary said casually as if she sensed the question before I asked.

I watched the room for a couple of minutes, observing muffled conversations between small clusters of wolves. I decided to go to the kitchen and get something to eat. It would probably be wiser to stay and try to mingle, but I hadn't eaten since last night.

The refrigerator was stuffed with food, but regrettably, it was all junk food. Obviously, I would have to change that. I opened the freezer. Nothing. I groaned loudly.

"If you truly cared for our Alpha, you'd leave." It was Lloyd.

I turned and nearly collided with his broad chest. His closeness startled me. I jerked backwards, managing to knock both doors to the refrigerator closed. He moved closer, his head and shoulders looming over me. I knew I couldn't simply react whatever way I wanted to. I was in a new world with new rules...most of which I didn't know yet.

He grinned. "Not so dominant now, are you? You want to call Rikki to come save you?"

"I-I don't want...please, back up."

He studied me, still grinning. "Or what?"

"Or I will snap your neck." Cecilia appeared in the entryway of the kitchen.

Lloyd snarled. "You don't like her either. Why protect her?"

"I never said I didn't like her. I don't know her. I don't like what she is, because it scares me. It is a threat to the pack. But the choice has been made and we must accept it now." Cecilia maneuvered herself between us, forcing him to back up a couple of steps. "I plan on letting our Alpha know what you have done. They aren't mated yet, but it's obvious to anyone with eyes how they feel about each other. It's a death sentence to even touch an Alpha's mate."

"Please don't," I blurted out. "I really don't want Rikki to... Just let him go."

Cecilia's ignored me. "Be wise and go."

He exchanged strained glances with both of us, scoffed, and then stomped away.

Cecilia balked and rolled her eyes as he disappeared around the corner. She turned to me. "You are part of the pack now."

I still didn't know what that meant, but I appreciated her help. "Um…thank you. Really."

She smiled and we departed the kitchen together to rejoin the others.

The pack.

I smiled a little despite the fears I had about trusting everyone. Cecilia showed me that my initial opinion of her could be wrong and that gave me hope, even for Lloyd.

Chapter Fifteen

Showered, fed, and relaxed, I was ready to catch up on a good book to read. I sat in the bed ready to indulge in a lesbian werewolf, romance novel. It fit the theme of my life now. The pack came to me throughout the day with questions despite Rikki telling them I was as clueless as them, if not more so about the fact that I was an Omega. There was a lot I needed to learn. They wanted to know all I could do. After the expecting couple came up to thank me for the fourth time, I was ready to hide in my room for the rest of the day. *My room*. I was already too comfortable.

"Meet me outside in 10 minutes," Rikki instructed. "And wear something comfortable."

She was about to leave when she realized I wasn't leaping up from the bed immediately at her command. I narrowed my eyes and snorted.

"Oh please, milady, won't you join me outside in 10 minutes?" Though she had a biting tone, one corner of her mouth lifted.

I shrugged. "Better."

I put my book down and got up. I sauntered past Rikki to the closet.

"*Midnight Hunt*," I heard Rikki whisper from a distance. My enhanced hearing was kicking in.

I chuckled, knowing she was reading the title of the book I was reading.

After putting on some yoga pants and a white tank top, I headed outside. I suspected the hunt was a training exercise. It was a bit disconcerting to know that this training was not simply meant for my assimilation, but also to ensure that I could defend myself. The rogue wolf and his thuggish pack were out there somewhere. A confrontation was on the horizon, rumbling in the distance like an oncoming thunderstorm. I shuddered.

Rikki stood in the small clearing in the yard, her arms crossed over her chest.

"Are you ready to hunt?"

I made no attempt at sincerity. "Oh, yeah. I've been waiting for this moment my entire life."

Rikki arched her brow. "Do you want to learn how to protect yourself?"

I groaned. "Yeeesssss."

She eyed me severely. "This is serious, Bonnie. You know that? Reading a fictional book won't help you."

"Yes, I am aware that this is serious. Give me a break, Rikki. This is all happening so fast, and I am not in the right headspace to shift."

"Relax. We won't be shifting today. Today is just about learning to control and strengthen your senses."

That seemed way more doable. I nodded.

Rikki closed the distance between us, and I blushed. She smelled so good. "May I?"

She stepped around me to face the back of my head. "I'd rather not have you brushing your hair out your face a hundred times."

As she spoke, she freed my messy hair from its loose ponytail. When her fingers combed through my raven locks, I stifled a moan. Every nerve ending in my body could feel each stroke of her fingers. I shivered when she spoke close to my ear. I might have prematurely orgasmed without warning. I wasn't sure. Being werewolf, every touch seemed more profound and purposeful.

"You are stubborn. And challenging me isn't wise. I want to help, so work with me." Her fingers curled into my hair and her grip tightened. This time I did moan, both my hands shooting backwards, pressing my palms into her thighs. I arched my chest forward, exposing my neck. This time, I knew my panties were soaked. My clit throbbed painfully.

Loosening her hold on me, Rikki went back to combing my hair for a few more minutes before pulling it into a tight ponytail. My body went cold, disappointed from the loss of contact. Whatever happened just now, had never happened to me before. Maybe it was because she was a werewolf. Maybe it was a skill honed over a long life. Maybe it was her ancestry. I could at least admit to myself now that I cared for her more than I had realized.

"You ready?" she asked, stepping back into my line of view.

I swallowed with some difficulty. My skin flushed. "Soooo ready."

I rushed past her and into the woods.

*

Our hunt was well underway. Sweat married dirt and rented spaces all over my skin. I was hungry. Definitely tired. The forest canopy shielded us from the worst of the sun. Most of the morning was spent refining my agility. Racing after wild hares was difficult enough, but stalking sinewy bucks was terrifying. Rikki was as feral as the wildlife surrounding her. Life exploded from each stretch of her muscles. Rikki growled, tossing a hare back into the bush.

Another 30 minutes had come and gone as I lingered near a tree. I was amazed at how well my body performed. Not once did I have to stop. I was stronger and faster than I imagined. I watched in stunned silence as Rikki caught a cougar with ease.

Jesus.

Rikki growled, pinning the cougar's head to the ground as it struggled against her grip. She was magnificent and strong. I kept my distance, not interested in getting to close to such a powerful creature. My fingers clawed at the bark of the tree when Rikki called for me to come closer. My legs would not move. I hugged the tree tightly when Rikki called to me again.

"I can't!"

"You are a werewolf, Bonnie. This cougar..." she lowered her head to look at the still struggling beast. "Let go of that human notion that tells you that you can't do this. You can."

There was an edge to her tone that suggested I didn't have too long to grasp the skills I needed. I had to push myself hard, not only for myself, and not only for the pack, but for her as well. Something was happening between the two of us, and while I wasn't exactly certain I was ready for a *mate,* I was convinced of my feelings for her. She was something special. Strong and untamed. But there were things that were necessary for me to figure out first. The most pressing of those was what to do about the rogues who were after me.

My legs found strength and I moved away from the tree.

"Come here," Rikki said. "I have it."

The cougar whimpered but did not end its fight to escape.

I swallowed. There was nothing pleasant about being near a hungry cougar.

"Kneel," Rikki ordered.

I reminded myself to trust her. Rikki wouldn't let the cougar attack me. I hoped not. Slowly, I went to one knee.

Rikki looked as if she was barely using any strength to keep it in its place.

"Look in its eyes."

My forehead crinkled in confusion, but I went along with it.

"Though it can smell you are different, you want to let it know what you truly are." As Rikki spoke, I followed her directions.

This was not the time for me to be a smartass or to argue. I thought Rikki was going to catch another deer, not a fucking cougar. It was perhaps for the best that she didn't tell me beforehand. She probably knew I wouldn't be okay with hunting cougars.

Instead of pretending to do what Rikki asked I was going to take this seriously. Narrowing my eyes on the hungry feline, I blinked repetitively, and I tried to straighten my trembling shoulders. I shook my arms loose and found the courage to fix my eyes on the animal steadily. Its orange eyes peered into mine. Its nature was primal. Ancient.

All I wanted was for it to stop resisting and to not harm me. After a few seconds, my body relaxed. My chest tightened as if something wanted to push through my sternum. Somehow, I knew it was my wolf demanding control. I raised my hand in front of me and spread my fingers apart. They were shaking. I forced my fingers into a fist and shook them roughly. The entire process felt like an eternity.

The first contact between my fingers and its fur sent a shockwave through my body. It was as if we were greeting one another in an archaic language known only to animals who were deeply connected to the prehistoric energy of the earth. It purred its approval and shut its eyes, accepting me. Accepting the wolf. We were kin.

I smiled involuntarily as I let my fingers explore the snout and neck of the cougar. I was exhilarated to be so near to such a powerful creature – to have an understanding with it. Rikki released her grip and I thought the cougar would flee, but it did not. Instead, it rose to his paws and brushed its body against mine.

"Come on, now. You are going to get hair all over me." I giggled gleefully.

Rikki chuckled at our interaction and watched as the cougar meandered off into the forest.

In an instant, her arms enveloped me. Her honeysuckle musk was dizzying. I pulled away just enough to meet her gaze. Hazel eyes met mine.

I cleared my throat. "Thank you for helping me."

Rikki's eyes remained fixed on mine in response. Her hand brushed the waistband of my shorts, and then gooseflesh appeared on my skin. I shuddered. I shut my eyes, desperate to regain control of myself, but my center was pulsating with excitement.

"It's impossible to keep a clear head around you." Apparently, Rikki was struggling as much as I was.

I tried to wriggle free of her arms to help us both maintain composure, but as I moved Rikki moved with me.

"I want you." Gold flickered in her eyes.

I wanted the same thing. But I wasn't ready.

"I want you too. I hope you know how I feel, even though I've not been so great at making my feelings clear. It's...well, you know, everything that is happening...changing now, and all at once, it seems."

She hugged me so tightly I thought our bodies might merge.

Her heart was pounding.

Mine was too.

"I understand. And I'm glad that you feel the same way."

Chapter Sixteen

Because of an angry outburst due to hunger the night before, I needed to go buy a new phone. It was a perfect chance to get away from the constant company of wolves. The errand only took a few hours to complete, so I was heading back to the house much sooner than I planned to. I had to drive a stretch of Highway 22, and on the way back, I was suddenly seized by overwhelming nausea. I pulled off to the side of the road.

The trees that lined the highway were so thick you couldn't see past them into the woods surrounding the area. Vomit gurgled in my gut and I realized immediately where I was – the scene of my attack. I swallowed air with great effort and stepped out of the car. I needed to end this fear. I couldn't let this control me.

I heard the familiar rumble of a motorcycle half a mile down the road heading toward me. I watched as it slowed to a stop in front me. I stiffened, worried that it could be *him*.

The helmet was raised to reveal Lloyd. He winked when our eyes met. "Hello, darling. Are you daring your wolf master to come claim you, standing out here alone?"

He was trying to provoke me.

"Following me?" I asked.

"How did you know?" He wasn't trying to hide his contempt.

If I could punch him without repercussions, I'd do it. I was getting better with training, but I wasn't yet good enough to fight with Lloyd, and it probably wouldn't be a good thing for the pack for us to be at odds.

I'd make him pay one day.

"What do you want?"

"I'm on babysitting duty. What I want is for you to head back to the house." He leaned forward on the handlebars of his bike.

Goddammit, Rikki. She had this prick following me.

I suppressed a snarl. "With pleasure."

I stormed off to my car with a new plan in mind: I was going to give Rikki an earful.

*

I blew across the backyard like tornado, full of destructive energy.

"You ass! You had me followed all freaking day and by that fuckface!"

I hadn't noticed that there were others of the pack gathered around the patio table. Rikki sat in between several wolves, providing me with one of her famous glares. If I avoided eye contact with the others, I could pretend they didn't exist.

"Well?" I asked impatiently.

Rikki stood from her chair, grabbed her glass, and downed the rest of her drink. By the sweet scent, it was wine. "Tato, would you please continue for me?"

"Of course, Alpha." Tato glanced at me. "Always a pleasure, Bonnie."

I stormed into the house.

I didn't wait for her to say something. "I get why you had me followed. But, why couldn't you tell me? And why did it have to be *him*?"

Rikki raised her hands defensively. "If I told you someone was following you, you would only get upset and cause a scene. And Lloyd was the only one available at the time to watch over you. He wasn't my first choice."

"The last thing I need you to do is piss me off right now, Rikki. You have to stop trying to manage my life!"

"I'm not trying to manage your—"

"You should have told me. Period. It's my life. My decision."

"Rikki." A man stepped through the sliding door.

I peeked over Rikki's shoulder to see who was interrupting our conversation. I huffed. We weren't finished.

"Give us a moment!" I screeched.

Last I checked, no one sounded like they were dying. I was more than annoyed.

The man arched both brows, as if it was me who was being rude. Rikki pinched the bridge of her nose.

"Mika, could you give us one more minute? Please?"

He smiled and nodded.

Alone once more, I spoke again before Rikki had the chance, "I think I have justifiable reason to interrupt whatever that was out there. You knew I wouldn't approve, and you decided to—"

"Bonnie," Rikki snapped. "I am trying to protect your stubborn ass. I warned you that you would not like some of my decisions. As Alpha, I have been trying to make the best choice for the pack as a whole, not just for you. You are not my only priority."

Her words hurt, but I was still riding the bull of my rage. "I never asked you to make me your priority. I don't want it! I don't need you!"

"Bonnie, you are taking my words out—"

"I think I heard you very clearly. You still lied to me and kept me in the dark. I won't apologize for being angry. And I won't apologize for saying, *fuck you*!"

I left her there staring after me.

I paced outside the main house and when I saw a car pull up, I decided to go for a run. I let my body guide me in my escape. Running was never a task. It was a way for me to meditate and find some measure of peace. A way to sort through my feelings by simply thinking of nothing but the air and movement of my body.

After 30 minutes of running without pause, I relished in my body's strength. I was not tired at all. I had a lot of anger simmering inside me and it was fueling my muscles. I wanted to keep running until I crumbled to my knees. I realized how far I'd run only as I slowed my pace.

Rikki owned a large amount of land. I rolled my eyes. How the hell was I going to get through this? I was stuck here. Pretending I could make it alone was unrealistic and dangerous. Freedom seemed like a fake word now. I didn't want to make myself feel better by turning Rikki into the villain. She was right. I was hard to deal with and I had been acting entitled.

Under the shade of the canopy, my existence rested solely in my sensations – the crisp air on my skin, the smell of wet moss on tree bark, the slow, steady sound of my breathing. It was perfect. I didn't want to stop. I wanted to keep running until I forgot everything that troubled me. Until I forgot Bonnie entirely.

For this time, I was free.

I discovered a grove with a small stream cutting through it. I stopped to catch my breath and to splash some water on my face. A sound disturbed my eardrums. Instinctively, I believed it was a threat. The hair on my body stood on end. My gut twisted up like a pretzel.

I swung my body around in the direction of the sound.

Snap.

Rustle.

I exhaled sharply. My wolf canines sliced through my gums. The shift was coming. The wolf in me wanted control. I knew it would keep us alive. I decided to let go.

I was fumbling with my clothes when I was suddenly shoved forward against a tree. Leaves were shaken free of their limbs. Two massive wolves were in front of me when I turned around. My eyes darted from side to side, taking stock of my surroundings. Stream, earth, trees. My options were limited. The larger of the two wolves shifted, and the human that emerged from the wolf was the man from my party. The one who claimed he had saved me.

"Don't be afraid. We are not here to harm you."

His companion remained in wolf form.

"What do you want?" I asked.

It was hard to avoid looking at his nakedness. He was supremely masculine. His earthy scent lingered heavily in the air.

He smiled. "Only you, my little Omega."

How the hell does he know about me?

I shook feverishly as he approached me. His fingers stroked my shoulder, and then seized a lock of my hair.

He sniffed my skin and then whispered, "You will be fun to have with my rogues. I will take care of that bitch's pack, one by one, until you are with me. You belong to me, and I always get what I want."

He took a step back and snapped his finger. The other wolf disappeared into the darkness. He smiled at me once more, and then was gone too.

I blinked rapidly in disbelief. I turned and Rikki was beside me.

"Were you harmed?" she asked.

I shook my head.

She heaved a sigh of relief. "I could sense something was wrong."

"Rikki." The stranger's voice was husky, but there was something melodious about it. It was the man whom she'd called Mika earlier. "May I speak to her?"

Rikki considered me thoughtfully for a moment, then nodded. She walked a few feet away, trying to give us some privacy.

He approached me cautiously. I'm sure he perceived my apprehension. "I am Mika. Family."

I finally caught my breath. "Bonnie. But I'm sure you know that."

"I do."

He was a dark-skinned man with light brown eyes. There wasn't a hair on his head, but his appearance didn't suffer for it. A pair of sunglasses hung from the neck of his shirt.

His scent was similar to Rikki's, but something was different.

He was human.

He grinned at my recognition. "You should use your nose more often."

"You are not a werewolf," I confirmed.

"Hell no. But Rikki is my mother."

What?

"My brother was a werewolf and a member of the pack before Rikki became Alpha. My parents were killed in a car crash when I was a baby. My brother adopted me. When I was nearly four, my brother was challenged for his rank and was attacked by three members in his pack. It bothered some of the white members to have a black man rank higher than them. He was killed in that attack. Rikki knew of my existence and came for me. She's raised me ever since."

Once again, I was speechless. Mind blank.

Rikki was a mom.

Chapter Seventeen

"His name is Cain."

It wasn't a lot to go on, but at least Rikki was able to discover the name of the man who approached me in the forest. The man who claimed to have *saved* me. The ghost of his presence refused to depart. His body, his scent, the sound of his voice. He was rooted in every corner of my body. Soil and roots. Moon and tides.

If Rikki detected my inner turmoil, she didn't give any indication. Her mind and her hands were focused on their task – making the perfect sandwich. She slathered a healthy helping of honey mustard on a slice of bread and then set about piling it high with deli meats, assorted cheeses, and small pieces of avocado. Once the masterpiece was finished, Rikki slid the plate in my direction and smiled. I took it gratefully.

"Why didn't you tell me you had a kid?" I wiggled the sandwich in her face in a chastising manner after I had taken a bite.

A smile threatened to manifest in the corners of her mouth. "Eat first. Then, you can come to my shed and we can talk."

Rosemary came into the kitchen just as Rikki was exiting. She noticed my sandwich and her eyes widened with desire. She pointed to it and pouted. I chuckled and offered her a bite. Normally, I wasn't a fan of sharing my meals, but I wanted to do whatever I could to integrate into the pack as painlessly as possible.

She closed her eyes and sighed with satisfaction as she shoved a large bite into her mouth.

"You make a choice yet?" Rosemary asked, wiping her mouth with a napkin.

My mouth was still full, so the only response I could offer was a confused expression.

"Whether or not to be mated to Rikki?"

Ugh, this again. "No. I'm still trying to figure things out."

"Like what?" she questioned. "I know I'm prying."

I mumbled under my breath.

"I only want what's best for the both of you. Your indecisiveness is making the pack squirm."

"My indecisiveness?" I said, a little louder than I intended. A few people turned their heads toward us, suddenly interested in our conversation.

Rosemary lowered her voice, which even I knew was a wasted effort around a bunch of werewolves. "I know you have a lot to deal with right now. Really. I get it. But you also have to try to grasp things from the perspective of the pack. Werewolves are almost always mated fairly quickly. We like our laws and our lines clearly defined, so we will all be on edge until you make a decision."

"I can't argue with you. We are both right, and we are both wrong." I put the sandwich back on its plate. "I'm tired. You can finish my sandwich."

I thought about going for another run, or just heading to Rikki's shed, but ultimately, I found myself in my room. I was determined to be alone. The soft cotton of the bedclothes welcomed me, and I curled up in them happily. I shut my eyes in an attempt to shut out thoughts of Rikki. The pack. The rogue. It was useless.

I thought of Rikki.

The pack.

The rogue.

I still had no clue exactly what I wanted, or how I was going to deal with everything. Anxiety mixed with my stomach acid and soured. Nothing was going to be easy again. The same again. I wrapped my arms around a pillow and squeezed tightly. Tears swam down the length of my face.

I cried and I was slipping – tumbling into sleep.

I took a deep breath and invited it to claim me.

It was night when I finally awoke. Groggily, I climbed to the edge of the bed and combed my fingers through my hair. I fumbled my way in the dark to the shower. I flicked the light switch in the bathroom and turned the shower on.

In the few seconds it took for the water to heat, I thought about Rikki. I needed a strong woman. A woman who could handle my own strength. And my stubborn attitude. Rikki certainly was that woman. It was a simple and not so simple at the same time. I really had no idea how to navigate a new relationship in this world along with the uncertain, impending future with the rogue and his pack. Regardless of all of that, I wanted to see her. Touch her.

I turned the shower off. I walked out of my room, down the stairs, out of the main house, and was soon facing the door of Rikki's shed.

I knocked.

The door opened, and Rikki stood in the doorway. She smiled when she saw me waiting outside.

"Come in."

She moved aside to let me through.

*

I yawned noisily as I stretched my limbs, the cool sheets drifting across my body as I moved. I opened my eyes and found Rikki asleep next to me. *That's right, I came here last night.* My movement disturbed her, and she rolled over to face me drowsily.

Rikki yawned demurely, covering her mouth with her wrist. "How do you feel? Did you sleep well?"

I nodded, scooting closer to her. The honeysuckle scent of her skin invaded my nostrils. Rikki leaned forward and kissed me lightly, her lips barely brushing against mine. My desire for her overcame me, and I snaked my arm around her neck and pulled her lips against mine in a deep kiss. Not satisfied, Rikki slipped her tongue between my lips to explore my mouth. I moaned softly, my fingers grabbing clumps of sheets.

I pulled away. My body was overheating. My wolf was awake. I was in need. There was an excessively loud pounding in my chest. I shuddered. My gums ached.

"Take a breath," Rikki whispered.

She combed her fingers through my hair and that only served to fuel the changes I was experiencing. I couldn't catch my breath.

"I can't think straight," I panted.

"Hey," Rikki cooed. Her hand cupped my cheek. "Your wolf is ready to claim me. That is what you are experiencing. And that's a beautiful thing. A mating bite is powerful."

I glanced at her thoughtfully, my arms still around her.

"Do you want this?" She looked at me hopefully. "We can just lay here."

There were a lot of things I wanted. I wanted to forget the night I was attacked. Forget about the time I threw up on a teacher I had a crush on in high school after being dared to eat three dozen chicken nuggets and spin in a circle. Forget that I was being hunted by a rogue.

Aside from all of that, I wanted to feel peace again. I hesitated, but I knew what I wanted. And it was Rikki.

"Yes."

Rikki smiled and a surge of electrical energy raced through my nervous system. I sat up, tugging at my tank top until I was liberated of it. My breasts spilled free. I felt free.

"Are you sure?"

I claimed her mouth in a passionate kiss that was suffused with a hungry fire I was unable to contain. I shivered with pleasure as her fingers softly teased the flesh of my lower back.

My lips charted a course down her neck. Rikki's breath caught in her throat. I pressed my body against her, the wetness increasing between my thighs. When I nipped on the flesh just above her collarbone, Rikki moaned, and then quickly flipped me onto my back in one swift motion.

My heart pounded eagerly.

"I am going to take my time with you, Bonnie." Her eyes were gold.

Rikki's lips closed around my nipple, sucking it attentively. My chest rose to meet her mouth, but I couldn't move a great deal. Rikki had both my arms pinned over my head. I squirmed as she switched to my other breast. My nipples hardened and my breathing quickened. Fire ignited in my belly, trailing down to my clit.

"Oh fuck!" I gasped.

Rikki was a woman on a mission. Her masterful mouth blew warm air on my nipple and I moaned loudly.

"I'm going to cum." My eyes squeezed shut, my body seizing as I trembled continually. "Rikki, you are killing me."

"Now you can imagine how you've been making me feel," Rikki replied.

I groaned, my body highly sensitive to the feel of her canines against my skin. My clit pulsed intensely. She continued dragging her canines down my body. I was so engrossed in each movement of her mouth I hadn't realized she removed my panties.

She raised her head from my belly. "Do you want me?"

I shuddered violently and nodded. I wanted her. Badly.

Rikki's tongue slithered deftly along the length of my thigh, working its way to my center. As her mouth found my core, my mind went blank from the magic of her tongue as she devoured me. Blindly, I reached with one hand for the headboard. The other entangled itself in her hair. She took her time letting the tip of her tongue flick upward against my pink flesh.

"Oh, fuck." I was panting wildly. "Rikki. God, your mouth."

Rikki groaned, and I screamed when her canines slid into the flesh of my inner thigh.

A Night Claimed

A few sensuous hours later, I lay in Rikki's arms. I didn't want to move. There was so much we still needed to learn about each other, but I knew then that we'd be able to get through anything together.

Someone was at the door. I could smell Rosemary on the other side.

"What is it?" Rikki asked aggravatedly.

I twisted to the side, half-expecting Rosemary to simply walk in without invitation. Rikki dressed and walked outside to greet her. I wasn't sure if it was okay to eavesdrop, so I tried not to listen.

"Send her through," I heard Rikki say, and then she reentered the shed and closed the door behind her.

I looked to Rikki for information. If she decided not to tell me, I wouldn't be bothered by that. I'd just go find out anyway.

Rikki chewed on her bottom lip. "Your mother is here."

I leapt out of bed and dressed rapidly. I knew it was ridiculous, but I kept thinking that my mom would burst into the shed at any minute and catch Rikki and me together. I reminded myself that I was no longer a teenager and my mom knew that.

"Are you scared?"

I wasn't sure if Rikki's question was rhetorical.

"That obvious, huh?" I pulled my jeans up to my waist. "There's nothing to hide. She will be happy for us. She's always telling me to put myself out there again. So…"

"Don't worry. I made a good impression the first time," Rikki assured me, confident as always.

I finished buttoning my shirt. "How did she know where to find me? I never told her where I was staying. Only that you live in Mill City."

"She probably came here and asked a local. This is a small town. I'm the only one named Rikki in Mill City who's a woman and owns land."

That made sense. I wondered why she hadn't called me instead.

I slapped myself on the forehead. "Shit. I broke my phone, changed my number, and never gave her the new one."

"She's not going to ground you." Rikki laughed, her hand covering her mouth.

"Try not to have the pack running around as wolves," I quipped sarcastically.

"We've allowed humans on our land before that didn't know our secret." She caught me staring at the floor. "Hey. It's going to be okay. Your mom will support us."

I nodded vacantly. "Okay. You are right. I need to relax."

I smiled and leaned in to kiss Rikki softly on the lips.

Rikki tilted her head to my side. "You are stuck with me. Don't you forget that."

"How can I forget? My body is still recovering," I whispered as we made our way to the main house.

My mother's eyes narrowed as she noticed my hands linked with Rikki's but gave nothing else away. I couldn't tell what she was thinking. She was processing now. She would make it known what she was thinking later.

A Night Claimed

I walked up the steps of the porch and slipped from Rikki's grasp to embrace my mom.

"Momma." I smiled. "I forgot to send you my new number. I'm so sorry."

"Stop worrying, Bonnie. It's not like I can ground you. But you did worry me. You weren't answering your phone. I was concerned." She wagged her finger at me.

"Yeah." I scratched the side of my head. "I have kind of been distracted the last few days."

"You've had that number for years," my mom said as if that was supposed to mean something to me.

There was an uncomfortable silence for a minute.

"Would you like to come in?" Rikki asked her.

I really needed my mom to like Rikki.

"Please, mom. Rikki knows her way around the kitchen. We could eat lunch together."

"Bonnie told me you were vegetarian. I make a really great veggie melt." Rikki was already headed to the door, opening it for my mom.

My mom smiled and nodded, then walked inside with us.

For the next hour I mostly listened and ate as my mom and Rikki discussed recipes. It was such a comfort to know that they were getting along. My family meant everything to me, and I wasn't willing to let them go.

Chapter Eighteen

The focus of the next several days was training. Strength. Agility. A lot of hunting. I didn't mind at all. I was teeming with energy – some of it could be attributed to the fact that I was a werewolf, but a great deal of it was due to Rikki. We were mated. I was still struggling with that concept. However, I was certain about my feelings for Rikki, so I was hopeful the rest would become a little easier to navigate with time.

Rikki and I had finished our training exercises for the day and were grabbing some food from the refrigerator when the couple who were expecting joined us. Izzy, the mother-to-be, waved to Rikki and me while she waited for Ric, her mate, to help her into a chair.

"How's your little girl?" I asked.

Izzy flashed a bright smile. "The baby bounces around a lot. It gets a bit uncomfortable sometimes, but it's better when I'm around you."

"Around me," I repeated softly. I had a feeling this was going somewhere.

She sighed and looked to Rikki for support. Rikki only nodded to Izzy.

"The last few nights have been *bearable*."

"Okay…"

She was certainly taking her time getting to the point.

Her timid expression did not help my own anxiety. "I get that being a part of a pack is new to you. And I am worried that you might find our request to be a little weird."

Oh, it is beginning to sound that way.

"I wanted to ask you if we could sleep near you tonight?"

"We could turn the living room into a bedroom. Rikki already has enough air mattresses to go around," Ric chimed in.

"Wait." I held my hand out. "You want us all to sleep together?"

"It's not a sexual thing." Ric sensed my distress. "The pack sleeps together sometimes. It's a way of bonding, of strengthening our ties as a pack."

"Well, *that's* comforting," I mumbled.

I wanted to help, but I wasn't thrilled about the idea of sleeping with people I didn't know very well. Rikki wasn't going to say anything. She wanted me to make my own decision. Looking at Izzy's swollen belly, I was able to sense joy from their unborn child. The baby liked me. I frowned, knowing that this arrangement wouldn't just be for a night.

"Fine," I said, giving in.

Ric and Izzy sighed simultaneously in relief. We discussed our expectations for a few minutes until she was ready to go upstairs for a nap. Tonight, we'd be sharing a bed.

"You could have refused," Rikki remarked.

"You know I couldn't refuse, whether I wanted to or not."

"You are allowed to say decline the request," Rosemary added as she walked into the kitchen.

"No, I couldn't. I don't want the pack hating me any more than they already do."

Rosemary was quick to reply, "They do not hate you. You are still getting used to them, and they are still getting used to you. I think you're actually fitting in quite well."

"I think so too," Rikki said. She held out her hand to me. I took it happily. "We are leaving, but we will be back later tonight."

I waved to Rosemary as Rikki and I made our way outside.

"Ready?" Rikki asked as she approached her car.

I smiled. "Definitely."

*

Mill City was a small town, but I had not yet had the opportunity to explore it. Most of my time was spent on Rikki's property. Tonight though, she wanted to show me around town. Well, not really around town so much as the local bar.

Banes Tavern reminded me of the bar in the movie *Road House,* except the employees at Banes were mostly women. The wood counters were long and L-shaped, separating the customers from the bartenders. There were several pool tables arranged in rows to the far right of the bar.

A woman with blonde hair and striking green eyes walked toward us carrying two drinks. She placed them on a small, round table where a couple was sitting.

She then turned to us and addressed Rikki first. "Rikki. I heard you finally got a mate. Didn't believe it until now."

She studied me critically and I narrowed my eyes at her. I wasn't impressed by her attitude.

She clicked her tongue. "No offense, honey. I needed to make sure you were good enough for Rikki."

The door to the bar opened behind us, allowing a breeze inside and enabling me to catch her scent. Human. I was surprised that she could be so bold.

"Well, you could just talk to me rather than staring me down."

She nodded dismissively and then returned her attention to Rikki. "Showing off our town?"

"Yes." Rikki squeezed my hand possessively. "I want her to love it here, Jeanie. Could we get a couple of those special sandwiches? We'll find a table ourselves."

So that's her name. I huffed when the woman walked away.

I inhaled sharply. "I want to poke her eyes out."

We found an empty table near the bar. My eyes studied the path Jeanie walked like a predator stalking its prey. The last thing I wanted to endure after everything I already experienced was some hag questioning my value.

Rikki slid closer to me, trying to block my view of Jeanie. When her hand snaked up the inside of my thigh, I gasped audibly. I was suddenly aroused, and in a public place no less. My eyes found Rikki's and I felt myself slipping away.

"We are mated. As a werewolf, it's natural to be possessive. She was rude, but she is human."

"Great. I'm turning into you," I joked through gritted teeth.

"If you weren't an Omega, you would have lunged for her throat immediately after her comment. I could smell her arousal. I am thankful you didn't notice."

I snarled and looked around for the woman again. She was nowhere to be found.

Rikki tried distracting me from the others in the bar who were staring at us, probably sensing the tension in the air surrounding our table. She was teaching me how to spot a werewolf without smelling them. It was a great lesson to learn. I guess we weren't out here just to explore. I was still training.

The old hag came to our table holding out two plates. "My specialty for tonight."

She smelled like lavender soap. I grunted. She looked down at me, concerned by my sudden closeness and walked off quickly.

"Bonnie," Rikki muttered my name, kicking me underneath the table.

I leaned back into my seat, scowling.

"What? I thought my shoes were untied." I couldn't admit to sniffing the old hag. She walked off and Rikki shook her head. "The old hag—"

"Her name's Jeanie," Rikki stressed.

"Fine." I slapped my hand against the table. "Jeanie. Whatever."

I stared down at my sandwich, hoping she didn't poison it. I was hungry and grabbed it with both hands to take a bite. I melted into my sandwich, wanting to savor every flavor that my taste buds experienced.

At least she can cook.

"Have you slept with her?" The question popped out of my mouth before I had a chance to think.

Rikki finished chewing and bit her lip. "A long time ago."

"How long ago?" I asked, the pitch in my tone climbing higher.

"Over 20 years ago."

"Did she know back then what you are?"

Rikki nodded. "Some of my pack are mated to humans. It's not an ideal situation, though. We can live for centuries and human lives are awfully short. So, I ended things with Jeanie."

"I don't think she got the memo," I said dryly.

Jeanie reappeared at the table to check on us. As much as I hated to admit it, my jealousy was uncalled for. I needed to work on my attitude.

I smiled at her. It was a bit forced, but I was trying. "Thanks for the sandwich. It was delicious."

Jeanie smiled. It was unquestionably fake. "Sure thing."

"Jeanie, can you talk for a minute?" Rikki asked.

She glanced around the bar and then nodded.

"I'm curious to know if you've seen any new wolves around?"

Jeanie moved closer to Rikki and lowered her voice to say, "There were two in in here a couple of nights ago. Looked like trouble."

"What did they look like?" Rikki asked.

As Jeanie described one of the men, I knew it was the man from the forest. The man from the night of my attack.

"Cain." I clenched my fists tightly in my lap.

Rikki's grim expression confirmed what I already knew.

"Anything else you can tell me?" Rikki continued her line of questioning.

Jeanie looked at me. "One of them kept claiming that you belonged to him. I think he was mostly trying to stir up trouble with your pack. Lloyd, Tim, Missouri, and Dana were here."

"They know better than to keep something like this from me," Rikki growled.

The fact that Lloyd hadn't said anything did not come as a surprise.

"What else?" I knew she was not telling us something.

"He did not fail to mention that you were an Omega."

Eyes were on me. Every pair of eyes in the bar. We were surrounded by werewolves. I shifted nervously in my seat as I continued to scan the bar.

Golden hues flickered in Rikki's eyes. Her fingers gripped the edge of the table and it started to buckle under the pressure. Whispers shot across the bar, and Rikki stood. The table never had a chance when faced with Rikki's ire. She picked it up and slammed it down with such force that the legs splintered and the center split.

Then it was silent. I'd never seen Rikki lose her temper like this. I reminded myself that as an Alpha her temper was par for the course. This may not be normal behavior for humans, but it was pretty standard for werewolves since their ranks were gained and maintained by their dominance.

"Leave!" she demanded.

Any humans that were in the bar scattered without resistance. The only werewolves left in the bar were her pack except for a few stragglers. One of them, who was clearly having a bad hair day, rose to meet her challenge. His chest puffed and he marched over to us. As he came closer, I realized that he was intimidatingly tall.

"Jeanie, go behind the bar," Rikki barked.

She sped off without hesitation.

I didn't know what to do. I'd never seen Rikki fight and preferred not to today. Another of the stragglers grabbed a pool stick from one of the tables. He broke it in half over his knee.

"You are not my Alpha." He pointed his stick to me. "And she shouldn't be protected. I thought we killed her kind off over a century ago."

I didn't want to challenge him. He was threatening me, and I knew he'd try and kill me if he could. His eyes lingered on me as if my mere existence was the most offensive thing he'd ever encountered. He hated me.

"You take one step and I will kill you where you stand," Rikki warned him.

His smug expression stirred the wolf inside me. "Alpha or not, I am older. When I'm done with you, I'll take your Omega bitch and take care of her myself."

I watched as he took a step forward, but he didn't take another. A knife sliced through his chest. It happened so fast that I didn't realize Rikki was wielding the weapon until I saw the blood spilling over her fingers.

The instincts that had been dormant in me for some time, those of a paramedic, wanted to rush to save the challenger as he fell to the ground. No matter who this man was, I knew who *I* was. Saving lives was my purpose. The wolf inside of me defied my wishes, forcing me to remain in place. My two natures were at odds. I never wanted Rikki to kill for me. And even though this could be seen as self-defense, it still felt seriously wrong.

The other werewolves to our left studied Rikki as if they were assessing their chances of winning. I hoped they wouldn't follow their friend who was now lying on the ground motionless. I couldn't take any more deaths.

"This is my territory. All of Mill City. I have been kind to werewolves outside of my pack. I've let you all into my territory. But no longer. Any wolves that are not part of my pack are unwelcome here. Leave. Now."

There was silence. Rikki took hold of my hand and pulled me behind her toward the front door of the bar. She pulled her phone out of her pocket and started making phone calls.

I wanted to go over to the man who Rikki stabbed and check his vitals. I tried to convince myself it wasn't my fault, but it was. Rikki wanted to protect me. It escalated so quickly I had no time to try to stop her. This is how people felt about my existence. They hated me. They were scared of me. Hell, I was scared of myself.

"Bonnie," Rikki whispered, the sound of her voice caressing my eardrums. She pulled me into her arms and kissed the top of my head. "I'm sorry."

She was sorry. That was funny. I was sorry. I'm the one who got out of that damn car, trying to play paramedic when I knew better. I'm the one who got attacked by some rogue Alpha. And because Fate famously liked to play cruel jokes, I was also an Omega. Something rare. Something feared. Something hated.

"I caused this. I can't do this, Rikki. I can't have anyone in the pack being killed because of me."

Rikki pulled back just enough to meet my eyes. "Bonnie, none of this was your fault. I chose to accept you, to bring you to my pack. I don't regret that. My pack doesn't regret it either. So, don't start worrying about things that don't matter anymore. You are part of us. And don't even think about giving yourself up to Cain. You know I won't allow that to happen."

"I would never give myself to Cain. But maybe I could leave the state?"

Her hand cupped my cheek. "You know that wouldn't stop him from coming for you. Trust in me. Trust in us. And in the pack."

"Most of them," I corrected her.

She nodded, and I knew she hated admitting that there were a few in her pack she didn't trust right now. Tato flew into the bar, Rosemary and Toni right behind him.

Rikki kissed my forehead. "Can you please go with Rosemary and Tato? I need to clean up this mess before I come home."

I appreciated her asking rather than ordering me around. I knew she wanted me to be safe. I wouldn't argue with her this time. Honestly, I couldn't wait to leave. The smell of blood was overpowering.

I nodded and let Rosemary take my hand from Rikki.

"Hey," she called to me as I turned to leave, "don't lose sight of how far you've come."

"I'll be at home." I smiled.

"Keep her safe," Rikki told Tato.

"*You* be safe," I said to her and walked out of the bar with Rosemary and Tato.

Chapter Nineteen

I climbed into the tub, partially submerging my body in the warm water. I brought my knees to my chest and buried my face between them.

"He did not fail to mention that you were an Omega."

Jeanie's words replayed in my head, stuck in a continual loop. I gripped my calves tightly.

I didn't want to be one of those women who thought giving myself up or running would save everyone else. That was unrealistic. The pack would still come for me, and so would the rogues. Plus, I still had to consider my duties as an Omega – Izzy, Ric, and their unborn child. Izzy could not bring her baby to term without me nearby. She and the baby likely would die.

A knock on the bathroom door wrenched me out of my own thoughts. It was Rosemary and Izzy. Their scents were unmistakable. I shouted for them to come in.

Rosemary entered the bathroom first, a concerned look stretched across her face. "You've been in here for a while."

There was a ridiculously ornate, golden clock on the wall above the toilet. I checked the time. I had somehow managed to lose over an hour in the bathtub. Worrying over impending doom could do that to a person, though.

"How are you doing?" Izzy asked, her hands resting on her swollen belly.

A Night Claimed

We weren't exactly friends yet, but she was awfully sweet, so I wanted to get to know her better. Izzy offered a towel to me as I stood, the leftover water winding down my body to meet the sea of bathwater. I took it gratefully and they left the bathroom to wait for me in my bedroom.

I set myself to the task of drying my body and slathering it with lotion. I wrapped the towel around me and joined Rosemary and Izzy in my bedroom.

Both were sitting on the edge of my bed engaged in light conversation. Rosemary stood and patted the space next to her. I hesitated for a moment, feeling as if I was about to receive a lecture. Nevertheless, I sat down next to her, knowing that whatever this talk was going to be about was inevitable. She surprised me by moving to a spot on the floor near the fireplace, stretching her legs out in front of her.

Rosemary and Izzy looked at me expectantly.

"I am scared, all right?" I blurted out. "I hate being scared. I want to fight, but I am afraid of who will get hurt in the process. Cain's arrival is unavoidable, and I know he won't come for me alone."

The door to my bedroom opened, and Cecilia emerged in the doorway holding a pint of ice-cream in one hand and a box of Oreos in the other. She looked at me and smiled.

"I thought you'd like something sweet," Cecilia said as she approached us.

I took the snacks and gestured for her to sit on the bed. "Thanks. It seems this entire pack knows the way into my heart."

"Yep." Rosemary giggled, her auburn waves bouncing against her cheeks.

"You're welcome." Cecilia found a comfortable spot to sit on the floor opposite Rosemary.

I dropped a few Oreos into the vanilla ice-cream and combined them the best I could. I got a few confused looks but no comments. Mixing ice-cream and Oreos together was a common enough thing, but I had no clue if it was common for the pack. I took a bite and let the cold, sugary flavors coat my taste buds.

"It's okay to be worried about Cain," Cecilia said. "I am worried too. I think we all are. My last pack…my last pack did not survive having an Omega among them."

"What?" I made no effort to hide my shock.

Rosemary and Izzy wore the same stunned expression.

"Only Rikki knows," Cecilia admitted. I passed the ice-cream to her and she began devouring it eagerly. "I, uh…Emily was my friend. We grew up together. Our Alpha was her father. He did everything he could to hide her identity as an Omega."

"What happened?" Izzy asked impatiently as Cecilia took a few more bites of the ice-cream.

"Well, you know, secrets never stay secret forever. The pack discovered that she was an Omega, and many of the dominant wolves wanted to *get rid* of her." Cecilia grimaced, staring into the ice-cream container. "It was surreal. They adored her one day and hated her the next. I did my best to defend her. Shattered a lot of bones on my end and theirs. And then…others outside of the pack found out. We were attacked by a large group of rogues and even a few of our own. Half of the pack was slaughtered, including the Alpha and Emily. It's been 40 years, but the opinions on Omegas haven't really changed."

A Night Claimed

40 years. It seemed like yesterday and ancient history all at the same time. The seriousness of my circumstances was not lost on me. But it wasn't only my concern anymore. The pack shared in my triumphs and my problems. The weight of my worry doubled.

"I was a rogue for nearly two decades when I heard about a female Alpha. I found this pack and asked to join. And I have only felt safe and content since." Cecilia passed the container to Rosemary. "Well, until you."

"Right… I am sorry," I said. It wasn't as if I didn't understand her feelings, but it did not make it any easier to actually hear the words.

Cecilia was composed. "Our Alpha has claimed you as a mate. It is done. I was meant to face this again. I don't hate you. Rather, I am scared to like you, to get attached to you."

Rosemary and Izzy nodded simultaneously. They apparently echoed her sentiments.

"However, you are different from Emily. She was a submissive Omega. That is why you have caused so much confusion in the pack. Those of us familiar with the stories of Omegas believed them all to be submissive. You carry the traits of both a dominant and submissive. But I think that may be an advantage."

"I hope so."

There was a loud growl emanating from the center of the house. It was Rikki.

*

I made it to the foyer in time to watch Lloyd being flung out of the front door, courtesy of an enraged Rikki.

His body sailed over the front porch and crash-landed into the tightly-packed earth of the driveway.

Rikki stomped out onto the porch, her body practically vibrating with fury. She pointed her finger at him menacingly. "I warned you."

Lloyd struggled to stand. "I never made a move against you or that—"

"Is that so? Would you care to explain then why several members of the pack have come forward to tell me that you have been very actively voicing your disapproval of Bonnie? Why didn't you tell me about what occurred two nights ago?" Rikki snarled, storming over to him.

Whatever semblance of arrogance that persisted in Lloyd after being tossed out of the house dissolved instantly. He lowered his gaze to the ground and there it remained. It was a few minutes before he spoke again.

"She's no good for our pack, and I am not the only one who feels this way. Nobody wants to offend you, me least of all. We…*I* think you are great as Alpha, but *we* also think that you are too lenient on those who do not belong."

Rikki's rage intensified. Her hands balled into fists and she drew them to her sides.

"How do you think we've come so far? Omegas taught us so much about our weaknesses and strengths. They are the ones who taught Alphas how to form strong packs and helped our ancestors to tap into our common mind." Rikki grabbed his chin and forced it upward to meet her gaze. "It seems that too many wolves have forgotten our history."

Several members of the pack, including Rosemary, Izzy, and Cecilia appeared on the porch to observe the ruckus. All eyes were on me. *What a surprise…because what else could this possibly be about except me?*

"I will not force you or anyone else to stay in my pack if they do not want to be here. I can ask another Alpha to take you. However, if you decide to stay you will treat Bonnie with the respect she is owed as a member of the pack and as my mate. Otherwise, I will cast you out permanently."

Rikki let go of Lloyd's chin and stomped off in the direction of her shed. No one moved. No one spoke. Even though Rikki was gone, the tension in the air endured. Following Rikki was my first thought, but I figured that it shouldn't only be Rikki defending me to the pack. I should also defend myself.

"I am painfully aware of how dangerous my presence is for the pack. Yes, I am new to all of this, but I joined because I wanted to. I wasn't forced and not one of you were forced to accept me. I will do whatever I can to keep our pack safe, but disappearing isn't the answer. The rogues will come regardless. The best chance that we have is together."

All eyes were fixed on me as I headed to the shed after I was finished talking. Rikki was kneeling at the fireplace, lighting the logs in the hearth. Her back was straight, her frustration plain to see. I rubbed her shoulders gently, and she leaned into the pressure of my hands. Seeing her this way was upsetting.

"We cannot allow dissenters. We won't survive as a pack if we are not together – of one mind." She sighed heavily. "Lloyd's opinion can grow and fester within the pack."

"I was amazed at your restraint with him."

She turned to face me. "Lloyd is an asshole, but he is pack. I do not wish to cause harm to any of my own, nor do I want to banish him. We need all of our pack. And we need you."

As soon as she was done talking, Rikki grabbed my arm and pulled me down to my knees. Her lips were on mine before I could take a breath. Our bodies were drawn together like magnets. I straddled her, our lips never parting. The growing heat from the fireplace was equally matched to the heat between us. I wanted to feel her passionate kisses on every inch of my skin, but I also wanted to taste her. For her to let go and let me lead.

Our kiss deepened as passion flooded our systems and we could no longer be gentle with one another. Rikki removed my shirt impatiently, her fingers grazing each patch of skin as it became exposed. Waves of pleasure rippled through my cells. I shuddered when her lips found purchase on my neck.

I was wet with desire. I shoved Rikki against the wall and set about unbuckling her jeans.

"Close your eyes," I instructed.

Rikki did as I ordered, but not without a smirk. I nipped lightly at her lips and then focused my attention on her jawline. Her honeysuckle scent was intoxicating. I pulled the rest of my clothes off and tossed them aside. Rikki opened her eyes, and I put my hand on her chest and gingerly pushed her back onto the floor.

"I'm in charge," I said, kissing along her shoulder blade. "Say it."

Silence was her answer. I looked up and saw that she was grinning. "I'm in charge. Say it," I repeated, but I secretly enjoyed this little challenge she was giving me.

Again, her only response was silence. *Time to play dirty.* Using the tip of my tongue, I blazed a path along her neckline down to her collarbone. She whimpered and I smiled. Rikki squirmed underneath my kiss.

"I'm…in charge," I repeated again, each word slow and deliberate.

I seized her left breast in my hand and squeezed it greedily. I wanted to claim her nipple and devour it, but I also wanted to drive Rikki crazy with anticipation.

Rikki slammed one of her fists against the floor, moaning as I blew hot breath over her taut nipple. Still I avoided taking it into my mouth.

"God damn it, Bonnie." She was nearly breathless.

"I am…in charge."

Offering her breast to me, she relented, saying, "Yes. You…are in charge."

With that, I finally brought her into my mouth. My fingers playfully twirled her right nipple. Rikki's arms wrapped around my body, her nails pressing into my back. Her legs opened and I slid my fingers between her thighs, delighting in the moist atmosphere of her center. Rikki gasped as I plunged deep into her. She moaned and rocked her hips against my thrusts. I knew she was on the verge of orgasm and I wanted to savor every sensation.

"Fuck!" she shouted as she came, her hands clutching large sections of my hair.

I withdrew my fingers, releasing a flood of sweet fluids, and then kissed her fiercely.

"Damn you," she said.

I smirked. I wasn't done with her yet. I went to my bag and pulled out the strap-on I'd been waiting to use with her. I kneeled in front of her.

"I need you to fuck me with this," I pleaded.

"Put it on me." Her commanding tone caused me to shudder.

I slid the brief harness up her legs. She lifted her hips to make dressing her in the harness a bit easier for me. Rikki's eyes were on me the entire time. Her fingernails grazed my arm. I waited for her to tell me what to do next after I finished. I was converted. I wanted to be dominated.

"How wet are you?"

Incredibly wet. I stood, naked and aroused beyond measure.

Rikki's fingers brushed my clit and I cried out, both hands pressed against the wall to keep me upright. My mind was foggy, and my legs were shaking.

"You want this?" she asked softly, her hand gripping the silicone dildo.

I could only nod, and she guided my body down to meet her. As the dildo entered me, I trembled and moaned, my fingers tangling themselves in her hair.

"Fuck."

Our breasts met. I rotated my hips as I moved on the dildo in a rhythm we both enjoyed. She matched my movements with thrusts of her own, which sent me rocketing toward an orgasm. I squeezed my eyes shut. Rikki buried her fingernails in my lower back, and then she commanded me to cum. And *fuck,* I did.

Sparks of pleasure shot throughout my body and I could feel myself surrendering to the beauty of our lovemaking. My body had never felt this content – as if every need had been met to the extreme. Rikki kissed my cheek and I shivered, gooseflesh forming on my skin. When my body finally went limp with satisfaction, I slid off Rikki, and then laid my head against her thigh. The dildo sat a few inches from my face.

"You are beautiful," she whispered, running her fingers lightly over my breast.

"I'm going to devour you," I announced. "As soon as I get some water."

"Oh, yeah?" Rikki grinned.

I ran to the small kitchen, grabbing a bottle of water from the refrigerator and took several quick gulps after it was opened. I returned to Rikki's side, kneeling beside her and admiring the angles of her body.

"Take that off," I demanded.

Rikki laughed heartily. "Yes, ma'am."

She removed the harness and put it on the floor beside her. I leaned in for a kiss and winced when she bit my lip. Blood sprouted from the place she pierced with her teeth. I pressed my mouth against hers hungrily.

I was headed for her belly when the door swung open. I was so startled I nearly shifted in defense.

"What the fuck, Tato?" Rikki hissed.

Rikki grabbed a blanket from the couch and tossed it to me. I wrapped myself in it and glared at Tato, angry at him for interrupting my time with Rikki.

Tato was shaking, overcome with anxiety. "I am sorry, but it's Izzy. The baby – the baby is coming!"

Chapter Twenty

I found the entire pack in the front yard waiting for me and crowded around Izzy. The birth of a werewolf was an event no one wanted to miss. If I was successful in bringing a cub into this world alive while also preventing the mother from dying, it would mean that all members of the pack would now be able to have cubs of their own. Something everyone here desperately wanted.

It was strange that Izzy hadn't been brought inside to give birth, but after thinking about it for a moment, I supposed it wasn't. These were wolves and were creatures of nature. Rosemary signaled for me to follow her into the center of the circle. I prepared myself to push through the tightly packed crowd, but the pack members moved aside as soon as I approached. At the center of the circle was Izzy, who was lying on the soft grass, and Ric, who was sitting beside her holding her hand.

Izzy rested her head against Ric's chest as a contraction turned her stomach to stone. She squeezed her eyes shut and blew air between her lips in an effort to distract herself from the pain.

There was no equipment available for use other than a medic bag. Rosemary had already started an I.V. of fluids for Izzy and had placed a small oxygen mask over her nose and mouth. The tank sat behind Ric in the grass. This was not going to be an easy birth. We were not in an ideal location and I could not forget the fact that Izzy was a human about to birth a cub. I rushed to her side.

"Where are the gloves?" I asked Rosemary.

Rosemary shook her head and held out the bag for me to see. "No gloves."

Shit. As a paramedic, I certainly wasn't unfamiliar with working in less-than-ideal conditions, but since this was an entirely new experience for me, all of the negative aspects of it seemed magnified.

"We cannot give or catch diseases," Rosemary explained.

"Talk to the baby, Bonnie. Listen to your wolf's instincts and go from there," Rikki advised.

That was at least some encouragement. I scratched my head anxiously. *Listen to the baby.* I needed to control my nerves. Today, a cub would be born.

My hands shook. I reminded myself repeatedly that I was an Omega. This was my purpose. I rested my hands atop Izzy's belly, feeling the contractions as they began and ended. It would not be long.

"You are impatient," I said to the unborn cub.

Rikki appeared across from me on Izzy's right side. She sat beside her and began stroking her hair as the contractions grew in intensity.

"Take slow and deep breaths," Rikki told Izzy, who was struggling under the squeezing pressure of the contractions.

My human mind was unaware of what my wolf was sensing and understood – there was old magic in the air that was guiding the process. As if Mother Nature herself was working through me. My flesh was covered in goosebumps. I could no longer hear anything of the action around me. My mind was clear.

I could feel the presence of the unborn cub, as if it were already outside the womb and next to me in the grass. The cub was ready. Impatient. Restless. Eager. Another contraction. The wind picked up, winding through tree limbs and leaves, its somber sound harmonizing with Izzy's pained groans.

Izzy pushed at my direction with each contraction. I lost myself in time. 40 minutes, two hours, 14 days – I had no way of knowing. A loud wail erupted. The sound of new life. I emerged from my trance, looking to this little bundle of pink flesh and amniotic fluid. *A girl.* She opened her eyes, a surprising hunter green, and searched for me in this new world. Once her gaze met mine, she recognized me immediately and began cooing happily.

I stroked her soft head with my fingertips. "Welcome, sweet girl."

Rosemary wrapped the cub in a blanket and gingerly handed her over to Izzy, who was anxious to hold her. Ric was crying and kissing Izzy's cheek.

His face still buried against Izzy's head, he said, "You have blessed us."

I knew Ric was speaking to me.

I could not help but be thankful for the fact that the baby was born without complications. Without the guidance of an Omega, I had been assured that this would have ended quite differently. The newborn cub would have shifted in the womb and tore her way out of the birth canal, ultimately killing her mother and herself in the process. I shivered and reminded myself that it had gone well. We had a healthy baby girl in our pack. We were lucky.

"Thank you." Izzy reached out for my hand.

I nodded, taking her hand in mine and squeezing lightly.

"Can you take it from here?" I asked Rosemary.

She smiled softly and gestured for me to leave.

I leapt up and raced into the main house. The bathroom on the first floor would serve as my hideout while I needed it. I shut the door behind me and walked over to the sink to splash some water on my face. I wasn't scared. I wasn't upset. I was mystified. I was finally beginning to grasp how much power I held. How much the pack would count on me in the future.

It was an entirely new identity rushing into my consciousness, meeting and mingling with the other identities that were cementing themselves as part of my whole. Human, paramedic, werewolf, Omega. It was a bit overwhelming. I observed myself in the mirror, almost as if I was waiting for the physical manifestations of these identities to suddenly appear in my face and body.

"You have done a wonderful thing today, Bonnie."

I nodded and turned to see Rikki in the doorway of the bathroom.

"There are so many reasons to fear what I am, but what I just did for Ric and Izzy...I feel more like myself again...like I am returning to the person I was before I was attacked, before I became a werewolf."

Rikki moved closer to me, putting both of her hands on my shoulders. "I am so happy to hear that, Bonnie. All I want is for you to feel comfortable with all aspects of yourself – the old and the new."

"I want to return to work. I can't let that part of myself go. What happened today made that clear to me."

"I know," Rikki said. "I promise, you will be able to return to work. But we have to take care of Cain first."

Cain.

*

The night surrendered to the dawn when the pack finally settled down to sleep. The arrival of the newborn cub excited everyone, and each member took turns holding, rocking, and singing to her. Rikki didn't need to tell me that it was their way of bonding with the newest pack member. I understood it was a wolf thing. I even took a turn myself.

The living room was converted for the night into a massive bedroom for the pack. Couches were pulled out, mattresses were strewn about the floor, and there were even some sleeping bags brought in from storage. Izzy, Ric, and the newborn were lying together in the center of the room.

I had a place of honor close to the new family, and Rikki remained next to me, her arm around my waist in a protective manner. It would only be too easy to fall asleep, but I couldn't close my eyes yet. I surveyed the room and my gaze landed on the new cub cradled next to her mother who was sleeping soundly. The baby's eyes were fixed on me. I smiled at her. There was an incredible bond between the two of us, one that would last throughout our lives.

I fell asleep with those new eyes on me.

When I awoke it was afternoon. The sun shone brightly through the window in the quiet living room. I opened my eyes to greet the rays of sunlight, quickly realizing that I was alone. *Where is everyone?*

I stood and stretched, deciding to go into the kitchen for something to eat and to look for the others. All I could think of was bacon as I raided the refrigerator – the smell and the savory taste. I hadn't eaten since yesterday morning. There were some frozen waffles in the freezer that I thought would be perfect with bacon, so I snatched them from the freezer door and tossed a couple in the toaster while I prepared the bacon on the stove. I listened to it sizzle in the pan.

A noise outside caught my attention. I turned off the stove and walked over to the sliding glass doors in the kitchen that led outside. Nothing. Not even a light breeze. *Strange. I know I heard something.* I opened the door and stepped outside. I closed my eyes and sniffed the air. It would rain soon. There was a wolf nearby.

The scent was wild and earthy. My eyes shot open and I grinned. *Rosemary.* She wanted me to come run together in the woods. Several others were close as well. Their scents were unmistakable.

I tore at my clothes hastily, throwing them in the grass as each article of clothing was removed. I smiled and invited the shift, feeling the familiar ache in my gums and refusing to struggle against the pain. The transformation happened quickly. Bones shifted, new skin and hair emerged, organs grew and rearranged. I was remade. I was free.

I howled and disappeared into the thick vegetation of the forest.

*

We were several miles from the main house when I became human again. I stood on my human legs surrounded by my brethren who had also returned to their human forms. Rosemary gave me a shirt and a pair of sweatpants.

"We usually keep a few bags of clothing out here, just in case."

Rikki was dressing as well, so I tried to sneak a peek at her body as subtly as possible. I was becoming quite possessive of her. She was beautiful and she was mine. The human part of me grasped for reason when it came to jealousy, but the wolf in me...well, the wolf didn't care. The wolf operated purely on instinct.

She caught my eyes on her and smiled. "Do I please you?"

I was certain the others had heard her question.

I blushed and cleared my throat. "Yes, you do."

Toni and a few of the other men were carrying firewood and coolers. There were camping chairs a few yards away.

"We will stay here tonight," Rikki announced.

"Yes!" Izzy cheered. "Did you like our game, Bonnie?"

"Game?" I asked.

"It's not so much of a game as a ritual," Rikki explained. "After the birth of a cub, the Omega would shift and seek out the cub, who was hidden by the rest of the pack. It strengthens the bond between Omegas and the cubs."

"But I only assisted—"

"You are thinking too much like a human," Rosemary remarked with some exasperation.

I frowned, not really understanding her point.

"That connection you feel with the cub? It's strong and overwhelming, isn't it?" Rikki was looking at me, but I knew she wasn't expecting me to answer her.

Tato snorted. "An understatement. Humans have the capability to bring babies into the world far more easily and using more avenues than werewolves. We only have the Omegas."

As I listened, I began to understand. "So, the game, or *ritual*..."

Rikki grabbed a soda from one of the coolers. "It is the final exercise of bonding between you and the cub. You will always be able to sense her emotions, her needs, if she is ever in danger..."

"And we know that this is not part of the tradition," Ric chimed in, moving closer to his wife, "but we wanted to ask you to name our cub."

I was stunned. "She is your first child."

"And now that we have you, we can have more," Izzy grinned.

I smiled weakly. "Wow. Well, I'd be honored."

A few laughed.

I studied the cub in Izzy's arms. She was strong. *Very* strong.

"She will be a handful. Capable of becoming an Alpha. May I hold her?"

Izzy nodded, and then handed the cub to me. The newborn stared at me with her green eyes, and I felt the bond between us solidify.

"Remy."

"Remy?" Rikki repeated in a questioning manner.

"Remy. I knew someone named Remy when I was younger. She was bold, honest, and fair. It's a perfect name for our new cub."

A small fire was made and then packages of hot dogs were retrieved from the coolers to roast. The sound of beer bottles and soda cans popping open and the light laughter caused by silly stories lured me closer to the middle of the pack – both physically and emotionally. It was a family. *My family.* Granted, I wasn't so thrilled at the beginning to be joining the pack, but who would? It was a difficult thing to be comfortable with for a person with even the strongest of spirits. But after today, I finally belonged. And now, Remy did too.

It was still overwhelming to think about the power in my gifts as an Omega. The position I now occupied came with arguably the most important duty – the propagation of the pack. Each wolf in the family wanted children, I knew. *Does Rikki want children?* She had never spoken about it, but now that it was possible, she might be more forthcoming about any secret desire for babies she harbored.

Rikki tugged at my shirt, pulling me down onto the thick blanket she had brought into the forest. "Come, sit with me."

I positioned myself between her legs and rested my back against her chest.

"You are tense. I can smell your anxiety."

"I was just thinking."

"I noticed," Rikki remarked. "Your forehead crinkles anytime you are deep in thought."

I peered up at her face. "I can't help it."

Rikki hugged me tightly and planted a soft peck on my hair.

"While you're *thinking* over there, perhaps you could also think about being the pack's healer?" Izzy interrupted, the baby asleep in her arms. "I can tell that you loved your work as a paramedic. You had a gift for healing before you became a werewolf. You should use it."

"We know you want to get back to that, but what about considering doing the same for all werewolves? Many others would love to be able to take advantage of your abilities," Cecilia chimed in.

"It's too dangerous for her to demonstrate her abilities outside of the pack," Rikki interjected, effectively dismissing the idea.

I was too curious to allow Rikki to shut down the conversation. "But werewolves heal exceptionally fast, right? What would I really be needed for other than birthing cubs?"

Tato, overhearing our conversation, joined our small subgroup. He took a swig of his beer and then said, "But there are circumstances when we cannot heal quickly or very well, and we would need further assistance. Historically, Omegas have also often served as a mediator between packs. You have so many talents."

"What could cause significant harm to a werewolf?" I inquired, suddenly afraid of the possibilities.

"Wolfsbane is poisonous to werewolves, and we cannot heal quickly with bullets lodged in our bodies. But when hurt, we are dangerous to be near and it's a risk to help. Therefore, many die. But as an Omega, you would be able to calm their wolves."

"She said she wants to return to her work as a paramedic," Rikki stated coldly.

"We all know that her return to the human sphere might not be possible. She is an Omega, and her gifts are far too valuable to the pack. Plus, she is more exposed out there than here with us. Other packs will come for her. We can protect her here." Tato's tone was argumentative, but I knew he wasn't trying to be disrespectful.

Rikki's eyes were golden. Her body shivered with rage. "*She. Will. Decide.* Is that clear?"

Tato lowered his head in an attempt to diffuse the tension and to show his respect for Rikki at the same time. "I know she will. I only needed to speak my piece, and to express what we are all thinking. It's not only her safety that concerns me, it is any human around her in her line of work. You know Omegas have great restraint, but when it comes to the presence of blood, they are just as dangerous and unpredictable as any other dominant wolf."

The looks on the faces of those around me confirmed it. I was a danger to others. My profession was not ideal for a werewolf, it seemed. The urge to retch was strong. *How can I not go back to work? How can I not be a paramedic?* I realized then that the reason Rikki was training me was not simply because I needed to hone my skills to prepare for the possibility of being attacked again, but it was also to train me to resist my bloodlust. Rosemary reached for my hand, curling her fingers around mine and squeezing lightly. I needed her hand. Without it, I was certain I would float away because I didn't feel attached to anything except the persistent desire to vomit.

It was all making sense now. Rosemary was able to keep her job at the hospital because as a submissive wolf, she would never lose control. But I was no submissive. I had submissive traits, but the dominant would always subdue them. The night I nearly attacked the man in the hospital made that painfully obvious. If Rosemary hadn't been there to stop me...well, it would have ended much differently.

Then, I thought about my job. It was a carousel of frenzied emotions and the appearance of blood was unavoidable. I couldn't pick the calls I received. What was I going to say to my supervisor? *'Sorry, but I can only work basic life support calls where I deal with minimum blood and only good people'?* They'd ask me to resign. I turned my head to the side, trying to hide the fact that I was about to cry.

"I won't ever have the control that I need in order to return to work, will I?"

She shook her head. "Not in this century."

I covered my eyes with both of my hands. It was not enough to stem the tide of tears. Rikki had spent so much of our time together encouraging me in my desire to go back to work, not once saying or even hinting that it wouldn't be possible for over a lifetime. I wrenched free of her arms and ran back to the house, not bothering to say anything to anyone. I left them there with their fire, their drinks, their new cub, and their bullshit secrets. I needed a break from this world of werewolves.

Chapter Twenty-One

I rang the doorbell of a house that I had not visited in a long time. My mom appeared in the doorway, and I collapsed into her arms like a little kid and began crying.

Minutes. Hours. Days. I had no clue how much time had passed since I rang her doorbell. I was curled up on the couch, my head resting in my mom's lap. She combed her fingers through my hair, and it felt as if she was detangling all of my knotty worries. My mother and I were never so close that we might be mistaken for sisters or friends. We bickered with each other constantly, though I never doubted her love for me. And whenever I needed her, she was there.

However much time it was that we had spent on that couch, it was all spent in silence. My mom never said a word to me, trusting that I would tell her what I needed to say when I was ready. Right now, I was stalling. I didn't know what to tell my mom. The truth was out of the question. *I am a werewolf. She could not possibly understand that, much less accept it.*

After my tears had dried and puffiness set in, I sat up to face my mom, knowing that I couldn't stall any longer. "I love my career, you know that. It's made me a stronger person and gotten me through so many tough times. But Rikki thinks I should quit. She believes that because of the trauma I've endured with this attack that it's emotionally unhealthy for me to remain a paramedic."

185

My mom did not speak right away. She looked as though she was carefully considering her words.

"What makes Rikki assume that?"

I sighed. I had to think of a way to tell the truth without revealing everything. "I... don't have control…over my actions, I mean. Not lately. I've…been having nightmares. Panic attacks. I'm afraid to even go into a hospital."

"Oh, honey." My mom pulled me into a tight embrace. She kissed my cheek. "I'm sorry. Why didn't you tell me any of this?"

I wanted to tell her the truth. I wanted it so badly.

"Mom, I'm just…scared. I feel like I'm losing my identity. Being a paramedic is a big part of my life, and I don't know if I can do it anymore."

"Bonnie, why did you come here? Not that I mind – I love having you here. But why aren't you telling all of this to Rikki?"

I shook my head. "She lied to me. She told me what I wanted to hear."

"I agree that lying was not very smart on her end, but shouldn't you let her explain why she lied?"

"Because she thought I was too weak to face the truth," I barked angrily.

"Bonnie," she said in a stern voice. "You have never been weak. I certainly don't believe that Rikki thinks you are either. Perhaps you should try looking at things from her perspective."

I didn't understand her meaning.

"Maybe Rikki was afraid to tell you because she knew you'd see yourself as weak. Anyone who knows you, knows you are your own worst nightmare. You'd start punishing yourself and taking it out on the world by distancing yourself from everyone who cares about you."

I was prepared to argue but I reconsidered. She was right. I was my own worst enemy. I leaned back against the couch. If Rikki had told me the truth right away, I would have closed myself off from everyone. No doubt about it. And the more I thought about it, the more I realized that I hadn't really run away because Rikki hadn't been forthcoming about the truth, but because I was terrified of the confirmation of what I already knew deep down: I couldn't just go back to my old life.

My phone buzzed.

"You should get that. It might be Rikki." She smiled encouragingly.

I nodded.

"Hey," I answered weakly.

My mom squeezed my hand and then stood. She headed to the kitchen to give Rikki and me some privacy.

Rikki sighed in relief on the other end of the line. "Where are you?"

"My mom's," I replied in a low voice. I wanted to make sure my mother couldn't hear me from the kitchen.

Rikki was quiet for a minute.

"I'm sorry I ran off," I said. "I needed time to think."

"I should have told you—"

"No," I interrupted her. "You were right to be concerned. I think I may have reacted differently if I had known sooner."

Before, I was still unsure about my feelings for Rikki. Before, I couldn't accept what I'd become. Before, I was holding on by a thread. Before, I believed because I *had* to believe, that I could return to my normal, human life.

"Can I come and get you?" Rikki asked.

I thought for a minute, then said, "Rikki, I need to feel human right now. Just for a little while longer."

Rikki said nothing.

"My mom is inviting you to dinner on Sunday. Come. And then, you can take me home."

"Okay."

*

My brother pulled into the driveway and I frowned. I knew Raymond wanted to meet Rikki again. The last time he met her, I denied there was anything between us. Now that I was living with her and claimed her as my girlfriend, he had all kinds of questions. My other brother, Shawn, would be here too. I was the oldest of my mom's kids.

"What's for dinner?" Raymond strode into the house, tossing his coat on the couch.

"Hang your coat up!" my mom shouted from the kitchen.

He rolled his eyes and took his coat to the closet by the front door. "Where's this girlfriend of yours?"

I squirmed noticeably in my chair. "She'll be here."

My brother wasted no time diving head-first into a lecture about my relationship with Rikki. A large portion of the speech focused on my recent change-of-address and how that looked to everyone. I had to control the urge to punch him.

I heard a car pulling into the driveway and I knew it was Rikki.

"Don't be a dick, Raymond. I mean it."

I rushed to the door. I walked outside and shut the door behind me. Rikki was walking up to the porch, holding a bottle in her hand. I thought it was wine but was surprised to discover that it was olive oil. And not a cheap brand.

"Something tells me you didn't spend five dollars on that bottle."

Rikki's wide grin stretched across the angles of her face. Her hair framed her cheeks in loose waves. She looked so beautiful.

I stepped forward to greet her, wrapping my arms around her neck. Our foreheads met and her free hand snaked around my waist. She kissed me softly at first, and then she parted her lips slightly, using her tongue to trace the border of my bottom lip. I shuddered with pleasure.

I reluctantly pulled away from her kiss. "You sure you want to go in there?"

"They are your family. I want to do this."

*

"Can we stop by the station?"

Rikki nodded without hesitation.

I faced the passenger side window and shut my eyes. Dinner had gone well, thankfully. My brothers could be assholes, but by the end of the night, they thought she was the greatest woman on the planet. With the threat of a rift between Rikki and my family gone, I was free to contemplate what to do about my career. I had to make a decision. Wasting time on false hope would only prolong the inevitable and worsen my pain.

We arrived at the station 15 minutes later. Some of the crew were in the bay, washing their rigs for the start of the graveyard shift. I spotted Jr. and waved to him as we pulled into the parking lot. He grinned and ran over to me as I was making my way to the office.

"You're not going to come by and say 'hey' to me?" His smile evaporated when he noticed my hollow expression.

Rikki had decided to stay in the car, knowing I needed to do this part alone. I appreciated her being here. This would be a hard transition for me.

There was no need to tell Jr. why I was here. He read my expression expertly. "I wish you would reconsider."

I shook my head, pushing my hands into my pockets. "I can't. I wish I could, but things have changed."

"Changed? Changed enough to make you want to leave?" Jr. asked, his distress was hard to mask.

I understood his unhappiness. We were the best of partners, and that was something that was hard to find. I went through four other partners before being paired with Jr. We had our own language. And now, I was leaving.

"I'm lost and afraid to do my job. I want to be here, but I can't right now."

"Fuck! Now I have to get a new partner. I wonder how many I'll go through before I find a decent one."

"I'll still be around, and you can always vent to me if you need to."

"I'm going to hold you to that." He hugged me unexpectedly. I tensed for a moment, and then relaxed into his arms. "I'm going to miss you, Bonnie."

I never thought a day like this would come. At least not for a few more decades. I turned in my resignation letter in the office, and then went to the bathroom to cry for a while. I wanted to stay. I wanted to stay. I wanted to stay.

When I finally made it back to the car, I could only apologize. "Sorry I took so long."

"Don't apologize."

It took us nearly an hour to get back to Mill City, but we didn't make it back to the house until later. Rikki got a call from Toni as soon as we drove through downtown. I couldn't hear the conversation, but Rikki's body stiffened as she talked.

We turned around at the next street and headed for Banes Bar.

Something was wrong.

"What happened?"

No response.

"Rikki?"

I cautiously touched Rikki's forearm. She jolted and the car swerved with her surprise. *Well, this is going to be fun.*

Rikki leapt from the car as soon as we pulled into the parking lot of the bar. She yelled for me to stay in the car. I was not going to do that, and I'm sure she knew it. I climbed out of the car and tried to catch up to her as she entered the bar.

A foul odor stung my nose as I approached the door to the bar and my heart throbbed in my chest. I didn't need to be a werewolf to know what that scent meant. It was death. I rushed inside to find tables and chairs strewn about in pieces. And then I noticed the bodies. There were several lying on the floor of the bar, their stomachs ripped open to reveal newly rotting organs. I didn't recognize any so far.

I spun frantically when I heard Rikki scream. I raced over to where she was behind the bar and saw her kneeling next to Jeanie.

Jeanie's eyes were open, but her body was lifeless. She was dead.

I knelt at the other end of her body. Rikki's eyes were golden and grief-ridden. She held Jeanie's head in her lap.

"It was Cain."

Cain. He was no longer in the periphery. Now, he was center stage.

She stood up slowly after gingerly laying Jeanie's head on the floor. "Toni!"

Toni emerged from the back of the bar. "Alpha."

"Gather a few of our strongest. We are going hunting."

He nodded and hustled out of the bar. I knew who they would be hunting. I wanted to help but I wasn't sure how.

"No," Rikki barked, sensing my intent. "You will stay with the rest of the pack."

Part of me wanted to argue. But Rikki was right and honestly, I preferred not to see the result of a hunt. I wasn't ready for that yet.

Whatever history Rikki shared with Jeanie meant a lot more to her than she let on previously. Rikki loved this woman once. Perhaps, in her own way, she still did.

"If you are going to head out to hunt Cain, you need to make me a promise first."

I combed her hair from her face as she raised her gaze to meet mine. She leaned into my palm.

"Anything," she whispered.

"Come back to me."

A smile was in her eyes, but it never manifested on her lips. I kissed her. I kissed her and she embraced me. I kissed her and the smell of bodies disappeared for a while.

The sound of someone clearing their throat broke the spell our kiss produced. It was Lloyd. He was staring at us blankly, waiting for Rikki's orders.

"Take Bonnie home. Protect her."

Chapter Twenty-Two

The atmosphere in the main house was tense. Most of the pack had gathered together in the living room and were mostly silent. I was sitting on the couch surrounded by Izzy, Rosemary, and Cecilia. They were taking turns holding a sleeping Remy. Lloyd was outside with a few members of the pack patrolling the grounds around the house.

I couldn't stop thinking about Rikki and the wolves she had taken with her. If the gut-wrenching scene at Banes Bar was any indication, Cain wasn't someone to be trifled with, and he had no interest in stopping until he got what...*who* he wanted. This is what Rikki had feared, and now I truly understood for the first time. Being an Omega was both a gift and a curse. I would always be in danger because of my abilities.

Lloyd burst into the room. His skin was caked with a mixture of dirt and blood. It was difficult to determine whether the blood was his or not until I noticed three distinct cuts on his right arm. He was out of breath.

"We have rogues here."

Time moved at a surreal pace. Everyone's eyes were on me, waiting for instruction. Rikki was not here, so I was the de facto Alpha as her mate. I couldn't shut down. I had to think of the others...the baby...

"Rosemary and Ric – take Izzy and Remy upstairs to Rikki's panic room. Once they are secured, I want Ric to return to the living room and we will make a plan."

"I can fight," Rosemary argued.

"I need you to protect the baby and Izzy, Rosemary. You are their best chance."

Ric nodded and called for Izzy to follow with Remy. Rosemary proceeded behind them.

I faced the remaining pack members in the living room. "Do we have guns?"

"Rikki keeps them in the garage," a wolf named Edward replied hastily.

"Okay, I need all submissive wolves to go to the garage and grab as many guns as you can. Then secure each window and door to the main house. Stay in pairs if you can – one in human form and one in wolf form."

Many of the wolves began talking amongst themselves, assigning roles and discussing their fear or excitement over the action to come. I was too focused on the next task to think of who waited for me outside. Maybe that was for the best.

"Where is Cecilia?" I asked, suddenly aware of her absence.

"She ran outside as soon as I came in. She's too stubborn for her own good and she's going to get hurt out there," Lloyd growled, tearing at his clothes. He wanted to shift.

"Damn it!" I threw my hands up in outrage. I should have expected Cecilia would do something like this.

Ric reappeared in the living room. His body was rigid with apprehension. He didn't want to leave Izzy and Remy, that was obvious. But he knew he could be of more use to the pack fighting with us instead of hiding in a panic room.

"Subtlety is not a strength of wolves. They'll come straight through the front door with the force of a battering ram."

I listened. I couldn't respond. I really didn't know how to direct the wolves. I was far out of my element. I was a healer, not a warrior.

Ric understood my silence and asked, "May I?"

I nodded, tucking my hair behind my ears nervously.

"Greenly," Ric called to Greenly who was loading a shotgun, "you and Nelia stand outside on the porch. Edward, Lloyd, and I will patrol the perimeter."

Ric turned to me. "You don't have to fight but standing out there with us will send a message. No one expects—"

"No." I grimaced. "I want to be out there. I need to find Cecilia."

I hadn't sensed Cecilia's presence for some time and dread was setting in. If anything happened to her, I would blame myself. I couldn't handle any more deaths. I should have kept an eye on her. I knew she was a stubborn wolf, so I should have known that she would rush outside impulsively.

Ric and Lloyd were shifting.

Edward smiled at me encouragingly. "We got this."

I hoped he was right.

A howl disrupted the quiet, night air. I recognized its timbre. It was Cecilia.

"Whenever you're ready," Edward said.

I nodded. I pushed open the door.

I looked at Ric and Lloyd who were already in their wolf forms. "Do not shoot until I make the first move."

There were 16 wolves of my pack at the house. 16 against an unknown number. The forest was black, concealing anything and anyone that moved through it. It was silent except for an intermittent breeze that disturbed several of the trees.

I detected movement near the tree line, and I froze. I raised my arms in preparation for a brawl but dropped them once I saw the figure of a wolf coming into view. Cecelia emerged from the thick, black blanket smothering the forest. She stumbled and was forced to her knees by the kick of an enormous boot. As the rest of the body was revealed, my breath caught in my throat.

Soil and roots.

Moon and tide.

Cain. Of course. The destruction at the bar was a sick lure crafted especially for Rikki. Cain knew she would search him out, and I would be left behind at the house under minimal protection.

"Th-This was your intent all along." It was not a question.

He shrugged and flashed a devilish grin. "I told you I would come for you."

In the space of a heartbeat I realized that someone in our pack was a traitor. Rikki and Jeanie's past was not common knowledge, which meant that Cain had been made privy to information that led to this moment. I stared at Cain from the porch. Cain returned my gaze. The link I felt with him was something so ancient and primal that my body shuddered with his closeness.

Ric and Lloyd flanked me, watching Cain and the few rogues that were walking out of the forest with a sense of dread. Cecilia was alarmingly close to Cain and was clearly in pain. It would be impossible to rescue her at this point.

My expression hardened, my cheeks nearly turning to stone. "Hand over Cecilia, Cain."

Cain snorted, his grin never leaving his face for a moment. He pointed to Cecilia who was still on her knees. "This one? No. We could have so much fun with her."

Well, it was worth a try. I knew who he wanted, though. Cain didn't come here for anyone else but me, and he wouldn't leave unless I was going with him.

I sighed in defeat. "I will go if you leave my pack alone and unharmed."

His eyes widened with the thought of his victory. He picked at his fingernail. "Of course. I don't care for anyone here. I came for *you*."

He was full of shit. He wanted me, that was true. But he also wasn't going to leave the house without sending a message to Rikki for keeping me from him. That message would be a violent one.

"You need to let her go," I said brusquely. I couldn't afford to let my fear show.

He took a step forward, his boots crunching the leaves beneath them. "Soon as you are in my arms."

Ric snarled as I slowly stepped off the porch. I held up my hand, warning him against any threatening movements. My shoes felt as if they were leaden. Each step required all the energy my body could offer. I cautiously eyed his rogues as I came closer. All of them were male. All of them were indistinguishable from one another. Each of them a statuesque Adonis.

I stopped when I was about 10 feet away from him.

"Let her go."

Cain licked his bottom lip, his eyes never leaving mine. He snatched Cecilia up from the ground forcefully and shoved her forward. She limped back to the house, never meeting my eyes.

I took another heavy step forward.

He grabbed my arm and brought me against his chest. His strong grip made me shriek and I bit my tongue in an attempt to keep myself quiet.

He chuckled as I squirmed in his possessive embrace. His lips brushed against my ear as he said, "You belong to me, Bonnie. Once we are mated, we will bring many cubs into our pack. Strong cubs that will subdue every other pack around."

Cain tilted my head and brushed aside my hair. He caught site of one of Rikki's mating bites.

A roar erupted from his lips.

"You *bitch!*"

I was flung forward with incredible force. Tasting alkaline earth and the biting flavor of grass, I struggled to rise from the ground. The familiar aching in my gums was a welcome sensation. My wolf desired control, and so I let her have it.

Cain was oblivious to the signs of my transformations. He was far too occupied enjoying what he believed to be his victory.

My canines were tearing into his throat before he could blink.

Unfortunately, he was quick to react. He took my shoulders in his hands and yanked himself free of my teeth. Without being entirely in wolf form, I couldn't do much damage, but I did enough. As soon as I hit the ground, I picked myself up and sprinted to the house. The roars of the rogues were at my back. Gunfire exploded from the house. The yowls of injured wolves echoed through the trees.

When my feet touched the front porch, I swerved around to survey the yard. Cain was ripping his clothes off his body to shift. The glow of his golden eyes was hard to miss. Another wave of bullets. I signaled for Ric and Lloyd to head into battle and then knelt next to Cecilia.

She was naked and shivering. I scanned her body for any injuries and didn't see anything serious. Some superficial scratches cut across her back. Probably from being mishandled.

"Get to the panic room," I ordered.

She snarled but said nothing.

"Please," I pleaded.

Cecilia grimaced but went into the house.

A rogue almost managed to surprise Greenly who was at the far end of the porch. Greenly caught his scent in time to fire his shotgun as the rogue closed the distance between them. I shut my eyes as blood burst from his body. When I opened them, the rogue wolf was lying on the ground, his head partially decapitated.

I never expected to see a sight so gruesome.

Another rogue wolf wailed as Ric tore into his neck in the front yard. I observed the raw power of Ric's jaw as it squeezed shut on the other's windpipe. I searched the yard for Cain, but he was nowhere to be seen. However, I felt his presence. He was here, somewhere.

Nelia, a member of my pack, was forced against a wall by one of the remaining rogues. An almost maternal protective instinct seized control of me, and I lunged at the rogue, ramming into his side at full-force. The rogue was disoriented from the hit, so I took advantage of the moment and kicked him between the ribs several times until he was removed from the porch.

The rogue fell to the ground in front of Cain.

His smile was wide, exposing his canines. Soil and roots. Moon and tides. Our connection was dizzying, and Cain took advantage of my foggy mind to attack. He didn't go for my neck, like I expected. His teeth sank into my shoulder. I screamed and writhed under his bite. I tried to free myself, but he clamped down harder. Blood poured from the wound and the world suddenly started floating away.

It was blackening.

Soil and roots.

Blackening.

Moon and tides.

Black.

*

I was thirsty. Definitely in pain. 100 percent *alive.* My eyes flew open. I noticed the familiar colors of my room and relaxed. Something must have turned the tide for the pack. Someone saved me. *But how?* A fuzzy figure came into view, becoming clearer as it approached. *Rikki.* She sat on the bed next to me, a glass of water in her hand.

"Drink." Rikki held the cup to my lips.

My lips seemed to part of their own volition, and cool water filled my mouth. I shut my eyes for a minute, savoring the nectary flavor of the water before swallowing. Rikki helped me to take a few more sips before sitting the cup on the bedside table. She took my hand in hers.

"Rikki," I whispered with some difficulty.

She kissed my knuckles and tears spilled from her eyes. "I'm sorry, Bonnie. I'm so sorry."

"It's not your fault," I stated matter-of-factly. I didn't want her to waste any time blaming herself. "Cecilia? Ric? The others?"

Rikki smoothed the blanket covering my legs. "They are all okay. Healing like you. Apparently, you were quite the leader."

I snorted weakly. "Hell, Rikki, I had no idea what I was doing."

"That doesn't matter now. What matters is that you are safe."

Rikki's fingers combed my hair, sweeping away errant strands from my face.

"Cain escaped. He sensed our arrival and he left. I don't know how many rogues managed to escape with him."

I grimaced at the sound of Cain's name.

"We captured two."

"What do you plan to do with these rogues?" I asked, already aware of the answer.

"*Question* them." This time when Rikki spoke, there was no gentleness in her tone. She wanted to kill them.

"Please, Rikki. No more bloodshed."

Gold flashed in her eyes. "No promises, Bonnie."

"Ask your questions. And when you're done, let them go or keep them caged until you figure out what to do next."

Rikki sighed. "Try not to think about it. The less you know, the better."

Chapter Twenty-Three

I remembered a moment during Cain's attack, a moment when his teeth penetrated my flesh, splitting sinew and veins. My mind was numb to everything else except the pain. Dark clouds concealed all thoughts. I was terrified that I would die, but what scared me even more than that was the possibility that death would not come for me then. That Cain would not kill me, and instead I would be forced into his pack, to birth his cubs.

I cursed myself for stopping, for getting out of my car the night I was attacked. I ignored every rational instinct and let my desire to save a life make me forget about safeguarding my own. I could have died that night. I *should* have died that night. But I became a werewolf. It *should* have been a second chance. Maybe it was. It was difficult to think of it that way now, since I knew that Cain would keep coming for me so long as he continued to live.

I admired Rikki's strength at a time like this. I was crumbling piece by piece with each minute that passed, and here she sat before me, stone-solid in her certainty. I knew it wasn't my fault. I kept telling myself that anyway. I didn't provoke the attack. I didn't even ask for it.

When I looked at Rikki, I realized how much I had been so inwardly focused. Jeanie was gone. Dead. Rikki had recently lost someone who was important to her.

Someone that she had once loved. I wanted to give her some indication that I could help to heal her. That I could give her love too. Softly, I brushed hair away from her cheek. Her nose crinkled, stirring from the sensation of my fingertips against her skin. I smiled and scooted closer to her. I shut my eyes and pressed my forehead against hers, hoping that she would feel the love that I was offering.

I slid my hand over her hip and grasped it firmly, then I allowed them to explore the space of her body all the way up to her hair. Rikki gasped softly.

"I am sorry," I whispered into her ear.

She hugged me tightly and buried her face into the crook of my neck and began to cry. I knew grief was a savage creature. It could break you apart and leave you unable to mend yourself. I kissed her hair and breathed in the honeysuckle scent of her skin.

"I will fight for you and for the pack—"

She kissed me.

We didn't need any more words tonight. Our future was clear.

We would fight. I would free myself of Cain. The pack and I would go forth together as a family. I wrapped my arms around Rikki tightly, confident that we would endure.

We held each other for the rest of the night.

*

"What happened?" Rikki growled as she rose from the kitchen table where we were sitting at the sight of Mika rushing inside from the backyard.

Mika was sweating, his eyes were crazed. "*He* came into *my home*! Took *my* girlfriend!"

The table was no match for Rikki's fury. It and the food we were eating were smashed to pieces. Luckily, I had gotten out of the way before I was smashed to pieces too. The chaos resonated through the house, and several members of the pack rushed into the kitchen, their eyes golden. They thought Cain had returned.

I knew this was not my fault and I couldn't make this just about me, but I couldn't help but feel some responsibility for all of it. I wasn't the only one being affected. I walked over to Rikki, gently pressing my hand against the center of her back. She stiffened for only a second but slowly relaxed into my touch. I wrapped my arms around her waist and rested my head on her shoulder. Her breathing slowed.

"We don't—"

I held my hand out to whoever had spoken, not caring who it was. Right now, Rikki needed a clear mind, otherwise she might rush after Cain without a plan and get herself and others hurt. We should have seen this coming. Though Cain was driven away the other night, it wasn't a sound defeat. So long as he lived, Cain would continue to come for me. In his mind, I belonged to him.

I kept my arms around Rikki. "You know what he's trying to do, Rikki. He's trying to draw us out to him. We have to come up with a plan. We can't just barrel in—"

"No," she hissed.

"Rikki, I—"

"No!" she yelled as she turned to face me. Her eyes were golden.

Desperation seeped into my tone. I needed her to listen before she did something foolish and suicidal.

"Rikki, we don't know where he or his pack lives! The only thing we do know so far is that they sometimes hang around Banes…but who knows if they will go back to the bar *now*?"

No response except the flickering glow in her golden eyes. Cecilia approached us tentatively. "Perhaps, we should listen—"

I slammed my fist down on the counter. "Let me handle this, Cecilia."

She was silent. Rikki was too.

I gave them each one more severe glare to ensure that my point was made. "Good. Now, it's no secret that he's after *me*, so I think we should use that to our advantage for once."

"Absolutely not, Bonnie. You are not going to sacrifice yourself! You think that's going to stop him? You think he won't lay waste to the pack once he has you?" Rikki's body was rigid again.

Damn it.

I knew I needed to remain calm. If my tone rose in pitch at all, it might set Rikki off completely and she'd be out the door in a heartbeat. "I am not going to sacrifice myself. I'm not naïve. Look, those two rogues you captured haven't given you any information we can use, so I think we need to devise a plan of our own."

She crossed her arms over her chest. The others held their tongues. "A plan? And what exactly would that plan be?"

I wasn't going to let her bait me into arguing. "We pretend to get into a huge argument. I storm out and drive home, followed at some distance by a few pack members. Cain is going to take advantage of that opportunity, and he'll snatch me from the road and take me back to his pack's den. Our wolves will then come back to you to report the location of Cain's hideout, and then you can plan your attack."

"You become bait?" Rosemary questioned.

"Exactly. This is the only way we can get Mika's girlfriend back safely. And it's the only way we are going to be able to defeat Cain. Who knows when he will attack next? We need to go on the offensive," I explained. "Tato and Toni should be the ones to follow. They are the best trackers."

A hush fell over the room. Everyone looked to Rikki for an answer, except for Rosemary. She looked at me instead. Rikki didn't say anything. Her hands were balled into tight fists.

"We both know you're going to do this whether Rikki likes it or not. And, it is a good plan." Rosemary shifted her weight from her left leg to her right. Her hands were on her hips.

"Are you sure you want to do this?"

I nearly jumped back a few feet. It was the first Rikki had spoken in several minutes. I was certain she'd still be seething, but I was glad she was actually listening.

I nodded. "I do. I can do this."

Rikki inhaled sharply, staring at the floor. "Okay."

I was relieved that Rikki agreed to my suggestion, and even more so that the others were also on board. This plan would work. I knew it. Cain was secretive, and it played to his advantage. To discover his den, someone would have to be bait, and he only wanted me. It had to be me. I shuddered inwardly. I would have to keep my nerves in check, especially when I was face-to-face with Cain. Our connection, our primal link, would make me highly susceptible to his influence…his presence. I had to fortify myself against it. I had to keep reminding myself of Mika's girlfriend, of the pack, of Rikki.

My nerves were perceptible to Rikki. I hoped she was the only one who noticed. She took hold of my forearms and our eyes met. My resolve steadied.

"I trust you." She said it loudly enough for everyone in the kitchen to hear.

I nodded shakily. "Okay. Let's do this."

*

Time doesn't drag its feet. It's impatient and moves ever onward without regard for those who must race to keep up, or for those who'd prefer to remain behind. I was the latter. Even though I had the support of Rikki and the pack, my nerves wriggled under my skin like worms working tirelessly through the soil of my tissue. The plans were cemented. Roles assigned and outlined. Each step painstakingly memorized.

The kitchen table had become a command center of sorts over the course of the day. A local map was laying open at the center of the table, horribly crinkled and stained with pizza grease. Balls of used napkins were strewn across the map where we had settled on the road I would travel. Cecilia put another slice of pizza on my plate. I waved my hand, disinterested in food at the moment. She nudged the plate closer to me, undeterred by my indifference.

"You are going to need your strength." Cecilia rested her head in her hand, her elbow flattening one of the napkins on the map.

I stared at the pizza. It didn't inspire any degree of hunger, but to be honest, I would have felt the same way about a perfect piece of prime rib.

I frowned and picked up the slice. "Thanks."

I groaned but ate the pizza anyway. Cecilia wouldn't leave me alone until I did.

Rikki wandered into the kitchen with a faraway look on her face. She spotted me and Cecilia at the table and picked up my glass of water and took several large gulps.

"Ready?" Rikki asked.

Chapter Twenty-Four

The cold air stung my exposed skin.

I had decided to pull off the road some time ago when I realized that I wasn't being followed by anyone except for Toni and Tato. It was quiet but not ominously so. *Maybe he isn't coming? No, that's ridiculous. He will come.*

There was a small bridge a few yards ahead of me. Leaving the car was probably not the best idea, but I was here to get kidnapped anyway, so I might as well pick a good spot to wait. I walked to the bridge, dead foliage crunching underneath my shoes. I sensed the presence of Toni and Tato. They were somewhere out there in the fog of blackness.

The bridge was made of a sturdy stone and overlooked a small stream. Large, smooth rocks crowded together at the base of the bridge, partially blocking the steady flow of water. I leaned against the stone wall, peering at the water below. I hoped that Rikki had managed to calm down. She wasn't doing such a great job of hiding her worry when I left. Now that the moment had arrived, I couldn't hide my fear either. I shivered against the chilly breeze.

Somewhere behind me, the sound of a branch snapping was carried to the bridge where I stood shaking with anxiety. The sound originated from a source that was close to my car. I couldn't see anything, but I could sense them. The rogues. They were here. A low growl resonated in the blackness. A lone wolf stepped out of the dark and onto the bridge.

I straightened my back. "I know you didn't come alone."

There was a loud *thump* behind me, and I turned to find another rogue on the opposite end of the bridge. I was cornered. Each of them took a step forward in turn, gradually closing in on me second after second. Their teeth were exposed, and threatening rumbles erupted from their throats. *I want to be kidnapped. I want to be kidnapped. I want to be kidnapped. This is fucking crazy. They are going to kill me. Why didn't I listen to Rikki?*

I shut my eyes as they inched closer.

"They won't hurt you, Bonnie. Cain would not like that at all."

My eyes flew open. There was a woman of surreal beauty standing in front of me. She appeared to be about my age and a few of her features were remarkably similar to mine.

She offered me her hand.

Why did it feel like I knew her?

"We must go. Cain is very impatient to see you."

*

I was blindfolded, which I expected. I also had expected them to knock me unconscious, but they didn't. The drive to Cain's den was relatively smooth except for the last few minutes. *It must be a dirt road.* I gripped the cushion of the seat when we hit a particularly rough bump. Tato and Toni were following, I knew. I was glad that they had managed to remain undetected so far.

211

A Night Claimed

The car came to a stop a few minutes later.

The woman helped me out of the car carefully.

"I'm going to remove the blindfold," the woman said.

I blinked repeatedly as it was lifted off of me, adjusting my eyes to the darkness. There was nothing but trees around.

"Follow me," she urged.

I followed, stumbling over vegetation. We were on a hiking trail.

It took us 20 minutes before the trail opened into a clearing. I observed the layout, realizing we were at a campground. There were several large tents that were the size of a studio apartment spread out in the clearing. It looked as if this camp had been here for a while. No wonder Rikki couldn't find a money trail of Cain or his rogues. They'd been hiding out here. Wherever *here* was. There were two different campfires roaring on opposite sides of the tents where rogues in human form sat eating and drinking. All eyes turned to me as we approached.

"Take her," the woman commanded. She handed me over to one of the rogues who had assisted in my capture.

He wasn't gentle with me. Grabbing my arm forcefully, he dragged me alongside him grumbling frustratedly. The tent to the far right of the campground was our destination. Inside of it were two large, iron cages. One was occupied, but I was pushed into the other so quickly I didn't have time to get a good look at who it was inside the other cage. The rogue retrieved a key from his pocket and locked the cage. He tapped the cage menacingly, then turned and exited the tent.

"You must be Bonnie," a soft voice said.

I turned to the cage next to me and narrowed my eyes. It was a little dark, but I could make out the figure of a woman. She was curvy and dark-skinned. Her hair was pulled into a ponytail.

I smiled weakly. "And you must be Mika's girlfriend."

She nodded, scooting as close as she could get to me in her cage. "Kesha."

"Sorry to meet you under these circumstances."

I wondered how much she knew. The last thing I wanted was to be responsible for exposing this world to her.

"How much do you know?" I whispered.

"I've been with Mika for almost three years. He told me everything on our fifth date. You're mated with Mika's mom, right?"

"Yeah. Mika told me what happened to you." Her voice wavered.

"Yeah. Well, I'm sorry I got you into this."

"It's not your fault."

*

Someone walked in and I knew instantly it was Cain. Soil and roots.

Moon and tides.

I felt dizzy, and so I steadied myself by gripping the bars of the cage as tightly as I could. The woman who took me from the bridge was standing next to him.

She snarled. "You swore to me you would never touch her."

Cain smirked. "Things change. She's powerful and needs someone like me to tame her."

"No one can tame me!" I hissed. I couldn't help myself.

The wolf inside me was awake and wanted control. She had been caged for too long. Her teeth sought to rip out Cain's throat. I stifled a snarl. It was no small matter to contain my wolf, particularly when I felt threatened or angry. My eyes burned. I feared I was losing to her.

"No one will try and tame you," the woman said. Her eyes met mine.

"Who are you?" I questioned, my voice gravelly with fury.

Her expression hardened and twisted in anguish. "No wonder she has come involuntarily. I trusted you to tell her the truth. You swore that you had nothing to do with her being attacked. You were supposed to bring her to me under friendly terms, but now I see that she is our enemy."

What the hell is going on?

Cain slammed his fist against my cage. "I am not in service to you, Braelin. You follow my orders!"

"You've had my loyalty for five years. You promised me that you would help me. This was all I asked for in all the time I've served under you." She shook her head and hugged herself. "Why did you do this? For a woman who doesn't want you? For greed? She doesn't even know who she is, Cain! How could you expect to get anything from her?"

His eyes were fixed on mine. "I'll shake it out of her if I have to."

A shiver rocketed up my spine, causing me to tremble.

Fear crumpled under the weight of my anger. I wanted them to stop. Stop talking about me. Stop making plans for me. Stop. I gripped the bars and yanked as hard as I could. The cage rattled, and I felt the metal of the bars bend under the force of my hands. It certainly got their attention.

"I am not yours!"

Cain hovered close to the cage, swaying slowly from side to side in a taunting manner. His eyes were golden. He sniffed the air between us, and I could sense his desire.

"I turned you. I have every right to claim you."

"Technically, you did not turn her." Braelin was trying to insert herself between Cain and me.

"Then what exactly would you call the attack that night?" I asked.

"I only meant—"

"Braelin!" Cain snapped, issuing a warning to Braelin. His eyes never left mine. "This would all end easier for you if you just submit."

I scoffed at his arrogance. "You mean it would be easier for *you*."

He deftly slid a key out of his pocket and held it up in front of the cage for me to see. He clicked his tongue and smiled. I thought he was going to open my cage. I was wrong. He strutted over to Kesha's cage and glanced at me before putting the key into its lock.

Kesha began shaking with such severity that I was worried she was having a seizure. I slammed my body against the cage door. I wanted to break free. I wanted to get his attention. Anything that I could do to save Kesha. I slammed my body against the cage again.

"Leave her alone!" I shrieked.

Cain laughed at my demand and opened the door to Kesha's cage. I slammed against the bars once more. I tried to ignore the pain in my shoulder. I was certain it was dislocated. Cain grabbed Kesha by her ankle and dragged her from her cage. She clawed at the bars. She clawed at the ground. I needed to do something. I promised to protect her, and I needed to do whatever I could to keep that promise.

I shut my eyes and called to my wolf. My fingertips tingled and pain snaked through my body as bone splintered and reformed. Claws emerged from the skin of my fingers. I pressed them into the flesh of my neck and grimaced as blood blossomed at the site of penetration.

The scent of blood caused Cain to release Kesha. She scurried back into her cage and curled up in a corner against the bars.

"What are you doing?" Braelin screeched.

"I will rip my goddamn throat out if you touch her!"

He glared at me with his golden eyes. "I dare you."

Blood spilled freely as I pushed my claws deeper into my neck. I suppressed the urge the scream. I met his eyes with determination. I was afraid for Kesha. I was afraid for myself. I needed Cain to take my threat seriously. Cain went to Kesha's cage and for a second, I thought he was going to grab her again. He didn't. He shut the door to the cage and locked it.

His expression was deadly. He would not forget this moment soon. "You have a choice to make. Choose me as your mate or I'll make the decision for you. I'll give you the night to think it over. Let's go, Braelin."

"I didn't know he would do this," Braelin admitted.

"Braelin!" he hollered.

She hesitated only a minute before disappearing outside with Cain.

Chapter Twenty-Five

I wasn't typically claustrophobic but being held in a cage for several hours certainly pushed me in that direction. There was no way to discern the time, but I could hear the songs of robins in the nearby trees, so I knew it was sometime before dawn. *Cain will be back soon.* I knew I couldn't give myself up to him, but I also couldn't allow anything to happen to Kesha. Resting my head against the bars of the cage I inhaled sharply. There was no answer. No way to win except to hope that Tato and Toni had made it back to Rikki and the others.

My arm was healed, skin fully intact as if my flesh hadn't been torn and bleeding only several hours ago. It was remarkable how fast werewolves could heal. How fast *I* could heal now. I shut my eyes from exhaustion, only now realizing how tired I was from all the chaos and lack of food.

"Bonnie."

Part of me thought I was in a dream. My eyes fluttered open, hearing my name called aloud. I looked over in the next cage and observed Kesha huddled in the corner, asleep. I squinted my eyes in the dark and shuddered from the cold air.

"Bonnie."

I recognized the voice this time. *Braelin.*

"I don't have much time. Cain is sleeping."

I stared at her, incredulous. "You want to help us?"

She nodded. A key was produced from her jacket pocket, and she unlocked the cage so swiftly that I wasn't sure she had even done anything until the door swung open. I snatched the key from her hand and hastened to Kesha's cage to free her. She was startled at the sound of her cage door rattling.

"Hey, it's me," I whispered, trying to calm her.

Kesha flew out of her cage and into my arms.

"Are we free?" Kesha asked, her fingers pressing desperately into the flesh of my waist.

"We are getting out of here, Kesha."

Most of the rogues were still asleep. We had to creep along in the cold morning air, being careful of our steps. Kesha had not let go of me since we left the tent, but she was holding my hand instead of my waist now.

Once we had reached a safe distance, Braelin handed me a flashlight. I passed it over to Kesha.

"When I tell you to run, do it. Don't look back and make sure you use the flashlight to guide you down the trail." I felt my resolve returning.

Kesha only looked back at me. She was ready to run. The silence between the three of us was short-lived. I heard leaves crunching several feet behind us. I could only catch the scent of one rogue. He must have been a dominant – submissives would never go hunting alone.

I turned to Braelin. "She can't go alone, not while we are being stalked. You have to take her back to my pack."

She frowned. "Fine. We will take one of the cars."

"What about you?" Kesha asked, concerned.

"Someone needs to distract the hunter. Don't worry about me."

Kesha squeezed my hand and then let go.

I heard the snapping of branches and I knew the rogue was getting ready to attack. I shut my eyes, letting my wolf emerge as a low growl rumbled in my belly. My hands balled into fists and I grimaced, feeling sharp claws pierce the palms of my hands.

"Go. Now!" I barked.

Braelin yanked Kesha behind her, and the two of them disappeared into the surrounding woods.

I shifted in the space of a couple of heartbeats and raced to meet the rogue who was stalking us. He charged me, but I was ready for him. I rammed my fist in between his ribs, and the rogue flew backwards into the thick trunk of a tree. My heart pounded in my ears. My breathing was heavy and ragged, producing fog with each exhale into the cold air.

His fangs were exposed as he rose from the ground, his golden eyes darkening. His thick paws crunched over the leaves. There was no human reason left. Only the primal. Only the instinct. Only the wolf. He launched himself from his hind legs and used his forepaw to swipe a hit aimed for my neck. I barely dodged his massive claws and stumbled. I regained my balance as the rogue's teeth caught my left foreleg, biting down through my wolf flesh. I felt the nearly fracture. I snarled as pain shot up my leg. I twisted my head and bit his neck, trying to wrench my foreleg free. It worked. He yipped and backed away, and I headed for the woods.

My stomach fluttered. The darkness of the early morning was giving way to the sun. I thought it was a good sign. Tato and Toni had made it home, and now the pack would be here soon ready to do battle and eliminate the threat of Cain and his rogues for good.

A low-hanging tree limb smacked me in the face.

A Night Claimed

I stopped to shake the loose tree bark dust from my eyes.

A loud *snap* spooked me, and I tried to run, but something around my neck wouldn't allow it. The sick sound of laughter forced me to remain in place. *Cain.* As I turned around, I realized that I was wearing a collar connected to a long chain. The end of the chain was in Cain's hand.

"When you act like a bad dog, you get treated like one." Cain yanked on the chain, dragging me behind him back to the campground.

*

The afternoon sun made the tent feel like a greenhouse. The air was stifling. Whatever strength I had left was spent on each breath I took. I hadn't really expected to escape but was stupid enough to let a tiny sliver of hope influence my emotions when I was running in the woods. I quelled the rush of oncoming tears, knowing that it would drain valuable energy to cry.

The tent flaps were pushed aside, and Cain sauntered inside the tent. He was angry.

"*Someone* is here for you."

I knew instantly he was talking about Rikki.

"I just wanted to let you know so when we are finally mated on a beautiful fur rug, you'll know whose pelt it is."

He was trying to bait me. I wasn't going to bite.

He scoffed and then smiled. "I'll be back soon. Then we can celebrate."

He left the tent and snarls filled the atmosphere outside. I shuddered. Cain barked orders, but the canvas material of the tent muffled the words. It had begun. I needed to trust that Rikki and the pack would prevail against the rogues. I needed to.

He returned a few minutes later with one of his rogues still in human form. He pointed at my cage. "Bring her outside. Use the collar."

I was restrained and dragged outside, my mind fuzzy and dizzy from the heat.

I blinked, trying to make out forms as my eyes adjusted to the light outside the tent. The rogues had shifted, except for Cain and the rogue at my side who still had a tight grip on the chain connected to my collar. I scanned the grounds in front of us. 30 yards ahead stood Tato and Toni. My heart nearly leapt from my chest. The rest of the pack emerged from the woods in turn, and finally Rikki stepped forward.

They were allowed to come within 10 yards of the rogue pack.

Rikki narrowed her eyes at Cain. "You know why we are here, Cain. Release Bonnie."

Cain snorted. "I'm not in the business of letting go of my property."

"But, is she really?" Rikki questioned.

There was a furtive look embedded in Rikki's stoic expression that Cain didn't catch. I did.

"He has a bad habit of not listening." Braelin walked up, arms crossed over her chest. There was defiance in her posture. She saw me and winced. "You swore to never harm her. I was foolish to trust you."

I hadn't taken the time in my capture to consider who Braelin could be. The idea of me being connected to her was not a thought I wanted to consider, so I put it out of my mind. I was good at hiding from my own thoughts. I only wish I had the ability to hide forever. But seeing her now, resembling someone I knew once, it was hard to pretend. I tore my eyes from her and back to Rikki, who had been watching me. My expression of confusion betrayed me, but Rikki said nothing.

Cain shook his head.

"I could have left you to be taken advantage of by so many dominants. I took you under my care and you," he pointed at Braelin, disdain in his voice, "turned your back on all of us. Your family. She is *mine.*"

"Is she really?" Rikki repeated.

I narrowed my eyes, trying to read between the lines. Rikki glanced at me meaningfully and I knew she'd learned something I was unaware of yet. I peered at Braelin.

"If you've come to challenge me for her, let us get this over with then," Cain said.

Rikki snarled. It was plain for anyone to see that she wanted this fight. There would be no talking her out of it.

"Wolf or human?"

"Human," he replied smugly. "To the death. And when I kill you...your pack will be mine."

The wolves made a circle in the middle of the campground. Rikki and Cain met one another in its the center. The atmosphere was thick and suffocating. My mind was foggy, but my eyes were focused on each movement of the two in the middle of the circle.

A roar.

A howl.

It began.

Rikki's fists met the tissue and bone of Cain's face with incredible force. He stumbled but did not fall. One of his rogues lunged forward to steady him before Rikki could land another blow. I tried to stand so that I might view the battle better, but a warning growl from the rogue holding my chain stopped me. I closed my eyes for a moment to tell myself that Rikki would win. She *had* to win.

I noticed one of Cain's rogues prowling the outside perimeter of the circle. He was searching for an advantage, for some weakness in the line of our pack.

"Watch the rogues!" I yelled to Toni.

Upon hearing me, Toni turned to meet the rogue behind him. He gnashed his teeth threateningly. It seemed to work for the moment. The rogue backed away a few feet. My rogue warden snarled his disapproval at me. I ignored it and returned my attention to Rikki. She had already sustained a few injuries, but they were nothing serious. Cain's leg raised to kick Rikki in her belly, but she caught his calf midair, and slung him into a nearby tree.

Leaves rained over their heads as Rikki slammed Cain's head against the tree. I shook with anticipation and anxiety. I was glad to see Cain weakening under Rikki's attacks, but I knew that my freedom wouldn't be won until he was dead. He tried to fight back but was unable to because of Rikki's relentless and hammering punches. A few of the rogues roared in anger, ready to join the fight.

Rikki jammed her claws in between his ribs. Cain howled and grabbed her wrists, then tried to pry them out. Blood gushed from his wounds, which only spurred Rikki to continue. She drilled her claws into him deeper, forcing more blood from his body.

A rogue leapt forward to attack Rikki. I struggled against my chain and was yanked back in place by my rogue keeper. More soon joined in the attack against Rikki, but the wolves of my pack were faster. Toni pinned a rogue underneath him and tore into his neck with barbaric intensity. I winced from the sight of exposed tendons and searched for Rikki in the messy scene that was unfolding in front of me.

"Bonnie!" Braelin's voice echoed through the crowd of fighting wolves.

Two rogues hopped in her way as she tried to run to me. She brandished a long blade and crouched, ready to fight. One of the rogues tried to grab her when she attacked from its flank, but she cut through the rogue's flesh with ease. The second moved in behind her while her attention was still drawn to the first. Braelin never gave them an opening.

Braelin moved swiftly, plunging her blade into the first rogue's neck and then twisted to slam the pommel of her blade into the second rogue's forehead. The first rogue died quickly, and the second merely staggered from the blow.

I could smell blood and death. All for control and power. I wanted it to end. I just wanted it all to end. I punched the soil beneath me.

"Enough!" I screamed.

No one stopped. No one heard me. Air filled my lungs and dissipated. I gritted my teeth. My wolf wanted control. I didn't want this. I didn't want death, or blood, or pain. I could feel the vibration of the wolf inside me as her heat warmed my body. Everyone continued to fight, their auras dark and knotted. Their energy flowed into me, and I realized then my true power as an Omega – I could manipulate that energy and use it to my advantage.

I needed to work quickly. I wanted to prevent more bloodshed. I could feel the Omega in me emerge as I immersed myself in the energies surrounding me. I connected them all together like weaving individual threads to create a fabric with a specific pattern. I was connected to all of them.

"Enough."

They responded to my command instantly. The wolves shifted to human form before my eyes. Confusion rippled through both packs, and the thick anger in the air evaporated into the glaring rays of the sun. This is what I wanted. I wanted the fighting to end. I wanted every wolf to submit.

Cain stood slowly, surveying the scene. Rikki rushed to my side and threw her arms around me. I was thankful for her touch. I was drained.

"What did you do to my rogues?" Cain snarled. He called to all of them, "Shift back!"

Several tried to obey Cain's command but found themselves struggling to shift. Everyone looked to me, understanding that I was preventing them from being able to transform. I stripped them of their wolves. Temporarily. I stretched my limbs out in front of me and watched as Braelin approached us. I was finally allowed to stand.

Cain stood motionless in astonishment. Hatred saturated the colors in his eyes. It was clear that whatever he sought to use me for no longer mattered to him. Quickly, he launched himself toward me and Rikki turned to protect me as they collided like Titans. Their exposed flesh glowed under the hot sun as each blow landed. Cain tried to kick Rikki's legs out from under her, but she was ready for him. She grabbed his leg and flung him aside. He nearly collided into one of his rogues.

No one stood to help him this time.

Rikki jumped on top, her knees buried in his stomach. A barrage of punches landed on Cain's face, his features buckling under each blow. Blood mushroomed from his wounds and spilled across his head. He tried to fight back, but Rikki's punches were relentless. Bones splintered, and the sound echoed in the circle. I turned my head to the side and vomited stomach bile.

As Rikki kept going, Cain's cheekbones caved and then his skull. Then he was still. Then he was dead. Cain's death didn't register with Rikki for a few minutes. Her fists continued their war with his face until I found my footing and walked slowly to her. With just a touch, Rikki stopped and rose slowly.

When the gold melted from Rikki's eyes, she pulled me into her arms. She ordered the rogue to release me from the collar, and he did without hesitation. I fell into her embrace and cried. Some of the rogues fled, but a few remained and offered their loyalty to Rikki.

I pressed my head against her chest and said so only she could hear, "Take me home."

Chapter Twenty-Six

I didn't know how long I had been asleep, but it didn't matter. I was home. I was with Rikki. It had been two days since Rikki had won my freedom with the death of Cain. The horrific sight of his corpse haunted me still, but I knew I was truly free. Rikki was curled up against my back and I giggled as she tickled me with light kisses on my jaw. She got on top of me and her hazel eyes studied me lovingly.

She kissed me. Passionately. Purely. Eternally.

Feeling her teeth graze my lip line, I moaned, wanting to taste her. She was mine.

"I love you." It was not hard to say.

She smiled, brushing her thumb over my cheek. "I love you too, Bonnie. You know…the pack is dying to see you."

"Are they?" I grinned, pressing my lips against her neck. I heard Rikki inhale sharply. "I hope they can wait."

Rikki shuddered when I slipped my fingers between her thighs and into her wetness. I rotated my index over her clit, and she gasped. Her hands gripped our sheets. Rikki moaned as I took her fast and hard. Her lips pressed hard against mine and I knew we'd need more than an hour to get through our mating frenzy.

*

"Took you both long enough," Rosemary teased.

I rolled my eyes and plopped down in one of the lawn chairs in the backyard. The firepit was lit and several of the pack members were roasting marshmallows. Rosemary handed me a marshmallow and a skewer. The atmosphere was entirely different. Cain wasn't coming to take me away.

Cecilia sipped iced tea from a pink glass. "I could get used to this. I think I'm going to sleep out here tonight."

"Agreed," I added.

"Remy loves the outdoors. I wonder what she will be like as a wolf? Ric says she's strong." Izzy kissed Remy's forehead as she nestled her against her stomach.

"She will be." I smiled at the little baby, happy to see her healthy.

"Word will spread that a cub has been born," Rosemary said, worry in her eyes.

"I'm not going anywhere."

"No, you're not," Rikki stressed, sitting down in a chair next to mine. "The Council has taken most of the rogues into custody, except for the four that wanted to join our pack. I think they might do well with our pack."

Council? What the hell is that? I also wanted to ask about Braelin but said nothing. I was nervous and unsure of what to feel.

As always, Rikki saw through me. "Braelin is one of them. They are on their way."

Rikki wasn't done. She had more to say. I could sense her stress, the wolf inside her pacing. I lifted my hand over my head, brushing my fingers against her jaw.

"Tell me."

Everyone around the fire pit watched cautiously. Rosemary had forgotten her marshmallow, letting it burn beyond recognition.

"The Council is coming too. They want to meet you."

"Uh-I," is all I could manage to say.

Everyone took that moment to get up and leave.

Rikki moved into the chair Rosemary had occupied and held my hand. "I won't let them take you."

"You think they will try?" I asked nervously.

"I am respected by most of them. They will ask. But they won't force you."

"Okay," I said slowly. I studied Rikki. "What aren't you telling me? What is this *Council*?"

Rikki grimaced. "The Council is a group of elders that rule on werewolf issues. It is an institution that was set up centuries ago to maintain order. There are a few members of the current Council that do not like me as an Alpha. I am female and have Native American ancestry. He...and a few others, are from the first colony. One of them was responsible for over a dozen Omega deaths."

"What?" I snarled, sitting up.

"His name's Luke. He joined the Council to redeem himself. But he still might harbor some animosity for Omegas, so we need to be careful."

"And here I thought we were finally in a good place," I said, bemused by the situation.

"When they leave, I'll make sure we all have a small vacation," Rikki promised.

Tato appeared in the doorway of the house. They're here."

Rikki rose and offered her hand to me. Tato walked out onto the back deck, Rosemary at his side. The pack reconvened outside, seating themselves in the grass around the firepit. Rikki would not ask them to leave. She would need their support in front of the Council.

Four rogues approached from the side of the house. One of them was Braelin. Another group followed – three men and one woman. The power in their scent was palpable. They were strong and ancient. Probably older than Rikki. I expected to see them in dark robes, but they were in everyday, modern garb. They noticed Remy first. One of their group, a man with silver hair, sauntered over to Izzy and Ric.

He appeared to be in his early 50s, but I knew that was bullshit. He felt too strong to be so young.

"It has been quite a few centuries since I laid eyes on a shifter child." He smiled politely, and I relaxed as he admired the baby. "May I?"

Izzy was hesitant, but she gave the man her baby. He cradled her gently and smiled when she cooed in his arms.

"She is beautiful."

"Yes, yes, she's incredible. Can we get on with it?" A man who I assumed was Luke approached the pack. "The child is proof that an Omega is in their midst."

His gaze met mine. I refused to look away in submission, and he snarled at my insubordination.

"Luke," the only woman of the Council said, "I thought it was clear, that your old ways were wrong. She has every right to be what she is."

"Damn right," I grumbled.

Rikki squeezed my hand tightly.

I frowned but said nothing else.

"As always, Rikki, you impress us with your ability to keep this territory safe," The silver-maned man holding Remy commented. "Despite all that, we are concerned for you. Having an Omega as your mate will bring you trouble, as I'm sure you know. Peace will be hard to come by."

"I appreciate your desire to keep my mate safe, but she is safest with us."

Her response didn't surprise him. "Then I suggest you make allies by using her abilities for other packs. You will need them."

Rikki nodded. "I will."

"Good," the older man replied. He studied me and smiled. "Our sanctuary will always be open to her."

"It was a pleasure to meet you," the woman said.

I smiled. "Same to you."

Rikki walked them out and I sighed, relieved to see them go.

"Wow. That was, intense," Rosemary said softly.

"Yeah." Greenly chuckled. "Luke *hates* you."

"I didn't notice." I rolled my eyes, thankful they were gone. "Well, enough of that. I think it's time for a vacation."

*

The night carried on as if it hadn't been disrupted by the Council. I managed to avoid Braelin for most of the night, but I knew I couldn't possibly avoid her forever.

"Go talk to her." Rosemary noticed me staring at Braelin and nudged me forward.

I groaned but got up anyway.

I was nervous as I approached. Tonight, the outsiders and I would become official members of the pack, partaking in a time-honored ritual. It would be a welcome distraction from the concern the pack shared that we still didn't know the identity of the traitor. The rogues couldn't reveal much either. Apparently, Cain was secretive. It made sense. It's the reason his pack thrived for as long as they did.

Frowning, I realized I was nervous. Braelin arms were folded inward laying in the grass, her head resting over her linked fingers. She tilted her head my way and smiled shyly.

Braelin moved to sit up but I gestured for her to stay as she was. I decided to lie beside her on the ground. The black sky was pregnant with bright stars. My skin hummed in harmony with the sound of the crickets in the grass.

I didn't know how to start the conversation.

Luckily for me, Braelin didn't seem to have that problem.

"You know, my father told me once that anytime I felt loss, the moon would remind me of who I am." She chuckled to herself and continued, "I thought his words were total bullshit. Telling me what I wanted to hear before he left me."

Her words forced me to think of my father and of everything I lost when he died. He didn't choose to leave me, but a loss was a loss, no matter how it happened.

"My dad was...a kind man. Honest and fair. He told me all the time that he would love me no matter what."

"Sounds like he was a great dad." Her voice was full of regret.

"The best," I boasted. Despite the alcoholism that caused his death, I loved him. "He knew I was gay, even before me."

"I'm sure it meant a lot to have his support."

"It did."

Braelin turned her head toward me. "I never meant to cause you so much grief. I was alone by the time I turned 17. That was about 30 years ago. I thought I understood life, but I will never understand why my father left me."

I reminded myself werewolves aged slowly. I would age slowly.

"Where did he go?" I asked.

Braelin smiled weakly. "The same place my mother had gone. To his grave. He was killed."

"Was he—"

"A werewolf?" Braelin finished my question. "Yes. The night my mother was killed, 10 years prior to my father's death, was the night my father and I were both attacked and turned. But he thought I was safer away from him and his new mate who was a trueborn werewolf and pregnant with his cub. I hated him for leaving me. Blamed the woman I never met. Blamed that unborn child. Jealousy is an ugly thing."

I understood that all too well. After my father died, I hated seeing my classmates when their fathers came to pick them up. I wished everyone misery, and it only made me bitter.

"When I found out my father was murdered, I assumed his new mate and unborn child were too."

"You don't have to share your past with me." I glanced at her and then back up to the stars, giving her the opportunity to change the subject.

"I honestly didn't care to know if they survived," Braelin continued, undeterred. "I became a rogue. Got into some trouble. Had a gambling problem. Was homeless a few times. Being a female werewolf alone in the streets was a dangerous thing. That's how I met Cain."

I perked up at the mention of Cain.

"About four years ago. Promised me security in exchange for my loyalty. He helped me beat my gambling addiction. And when my mind was finally clean, I told him about my father and his mate and unborn child. He got curious and had me share everything I knew. And one day, he came and told me I had a sister. He said that her mother was also killed, and the baby was taken and hidden with a human family."

I said nothing.

"It took me a few more years to let go of all the pain left in my heart. And that is when I pleaded with Cain to help me find her. I wanted to make things right. I'd let her down before and couldn't do it again. I knew, one day, she would need me." Braelin pulled handfuls of grass from the earth. "I didn't know Cain had a hidden agenda."

I stood abruptly. "I don't want to talk about this. This is—"

"Bonnie."

"I said, I don't want to talk about this anymore!" I yelled.

Braelin tried to reach out but I took a step back. "Bonnie. You feel a connection with me. You felt it the moment we met. And you see the resemblance."

I shook my head. "No. It doesn't make sense. I have been human all my life."

"History proves that a born cub doesn't shift until their late teens. Maybe you were a late bloomer? Cain only wanted to induce your shift, but he never caused you to turn. You can't turn a born werewolf."

"No!" I yelled again.

234

I noticed Rikki approaching. The pack was inside the house. I rushed to Rikki, feeling the tears forming in my eyes.

"She has to be wrong! My mom would never lie to me! People have always told me how much we all look alike!"

"And you should," Braelin remarked. "When Rikki told me who your parents were, that made sense. I had a little sister. I don't know how he found her, but he thought it was best to give you to her."

"What?" I laughed, not wanting to believe her story. "You're telling me, the woman who raised me is my...sister? That you are my sister? And I was born through two werewolves, which is very rare? And my brothers are my nephews? And she kept this all from me?"

"Yes," Braelin said calmly. "Except, she doesn't know the truth about you. However, they adopted you. I don't know why. I doubt she even remembers me."

I couldn't be sure if the ground was still under my feet. The stars blurred together in my view, and the trees became a sea of hunter green. I wanted to cry and scream and shake, anything to remove the last few minutes from existence. But I knew that was futile. There was nothing that could erase this moment. Nothing that could slip the grasp of Truth when it had you in its suffocating embrace.

Everything I had known was gone. All that I was...gone. And though Braelin had given me so much information, I still had a million questions. I didn't want to ask any of them now. The ache in my gums and familiar agony of the shift overcame me.

I left them there staring after me.

A Night Claimed

I ran.

I ran into the woods and felt them getting smaller behind me.

Me. Did I have any idea who that was?

I surrendered to the wolf inside me, knowing that I would be comfortable in that identity for a while. Bonnie was gone. Only the wolf remained.

Epilogue

The need to shift was strong. My wolf lurked close to the surface of my skin, impatient for the full moon to reach its zenith. A black blanket of sky stretched across the dome of the Earth. Starlight flooded the area, refusing to rob the forest of its vibrant, green hues. The chirping of crickets echoed through the darkness. It was peaceful. I was ready.

Tonight, I would officially become a member of the pack.

"We will hunt, and you will lead. It is our way of welcoming you into the pack and solidifying the bond between all of us," Toni explained.

I smiled in anticipation. Braelin and the other three rogues would also lead their own hunting parties. They would no longer be rogues. They would be pack. *We* would be family. They seemed as eager to belong as I was, and I felt happy for the four of them.

It was difficult to interact with Braelin, but I knew that I had to put away my feelings for the moment because this night was far too important for both of us. When I approached her, my legs started trembling and I had to steady myself. *Just talk to her, Bonnie*

I cleared my throat and she turned around to face me. "I...Um..."

I dropped my head in defeat. *What the hell am I going to say?*

Luckily for me, Braelin spoke up, saying, "It's okay. It took me almost 30 years before I was ready to face you. I thought I'd just make sure you were safe and leave you alone, but then about two years ago, I realized that I really wanted to get to know you." She smiled and that seemed to ease the tension in the air between us. "You're entitled to be skeptical of me and of our history. I probably would be too if I was in your position."

I shook my head.

"That isn't it." I sighed. "I'm...not a fan of change, especially when it's an earth-shattering change. I don't handle it well."

"Fair enough."

"I'm not saying that I don't want to know you. I mean, I—"

Braelin held up both of her hands and smiled. "Relax."

I noticed that my claws had emerged. I attributed it to the stress of our discussion plus the impending full moon. "I'll never get use to this."

"Yes, you will." Braelin reached out and squeezed my clawed hand. "Give yourself time."

Arms wrapped around my waist and hugged me tightly. The scent of honeysuckle was overpowering. *Rikki.*

She leaned her head over my shoulder to kiss my cheek. "You smell like you are ready to shift."

"I am. And, I'm ready to belong to this pack." I shot a glance at Braelin.

*

There was a lot for me to process, and I'm certain that there would be more surprises for me in the future. There were also so many decisions I needed to make. I needed to talk to my mom about Braelin and our shared history. I simply could not go on as before without that being cleared up, and maybe it would make things better to have Braelin included in our family unit.

It was difficult not to wonder what my life might have been like had I been raised as a werewolf, knowing my identity. Rikki wanted me to keep all of that secret for now. I understood. The pack and I still needed to grapple with my identity as an Omega. But it would not stop me from searching for all of the answers I desperately wanted. I wanted to know more about my birth parents, for starters, and more about the history of my family. I knew those answers would come in time.

Once the hunt was over, the pack rested together around a campfire in a clearing in the forest. Rikki wrapped a blanket around me, and we snuggled together while listening to the crackle and hiss of the fire. Everyone was quiet and content. I closed my eyes, ready for sleep.

I felt something buzzing at my backside, and then felt Rikki reach between us to pull out a phone.

"Yes," she answered.

I could sense Rikki's anxiety as she spoke with whoever was on the other end of the line. I was not the only one – most of the pack had turned their attention toward us. She stiffened, then put the phone down on the ground.

"What's up? Toni asked.

"The Council has already announced that we have an Omega and a cub. It seems they didn't want to wait."

Rikki agitatedly combed her fingers through her brunette hair. "That was the Alpha in Mount Angel. He is on his way here now. He needs our help."

I thought I had more time to adjust, to be hidden from the rest of the supernatural world. I was wrong. But there was a strain in Rikki's tone that troubled me more than the news that I was no longer anonymous to other packs. Trouble would be following this Alpha. I knew it. It would be trouble that I could not avoid. I was comforted somewhat in the knowledge that I was no longer alone.

For the first time, I was thankful to Cain. He may not have turned me into a werewolf, but he had changed my life forever and even brought me to Rikki. I'd be lost without her. I had more now than I ever thought I'd need. And I would show my own appreciation to my mate tonight when I made love to her in these woods. I was a part of this strange and extraordinary world and I would no longer run from it.

I snuggled closer to Rikki and she wrapped her arm around me.

There would be peace for a little while. And that's all I needed in that moment.

About the Author

Domina Alexandra is a native of Southern California who has recently transplanted to Salem, Oregon. She is an author of stories with strong female protagonists, authentic emotions and thrilling action scenes that mirror her career as an EMT on the way to becoming a SWAT Medic. She grew up writing poetry as an outlet and, in 2006, joined a Live Theater program, where she played many roles in productions of plays and musicals. During her four years of acting, she fell in love with writing monologues, screenplays, and all things story. When she's not saving lives as an EMT, she advocates for LGBT Youth with a vision of growing a stronger community of care, acceptance, and compassion. Her books include *Her Endure* and *I Belong With Her*. She gets her imaginative ideas from her life as a EMT as well as being stuck in her head too long as a child.

Other Titles Available From Triplicity Publishing

Deadly Deception by Cade Brogan. Three die in a psychiatric hospital. A triple homicide. A contagion, deadly and mysterious, is the killer's weapon of choice. A dart flies. A woman dies in the shower, her neck punctured. A homicide, hours from Chicago. Poison, deadly and concocted, is the killer's weapon of choice. As her city teeters on the verge of panic, Detective Rylee Hayes is forced to divide her attention between two killers—one whose actions could result in a global pandemic and the other, an old nemesis, whose next target is her fiancée. And the clock ticks down…

Stunted by Breanna Hughes. Professional stuntwoman Jessie Knight takes her job very seriously and although she works in the entertainment industry, she has zero desire for fame or notoriety. She also has a very strict no-dating policy when it comes to coworkers. That is, until, she meets famous actress Elliot Chase on the set of her new film. The adrenaline rush of the stunts is nothing compared to the sparks that fly between them. After a passionate night together, a sex tape is leaked that sends Jessie and Elliot's private and professional lives into a spiral. Will the fallout be too much for them to last? Or will they find a way out of the mess together?

Mission Compromised by Graysen Morgen. Natalia Moreno is thrilled when she arrives in Fiji for a relaxing vacation. However, she soon discovers the overwater bungalow she's staying in has been double booked for the entire stay, and the resort is full. Annoyed and frustrated, she has no other choice but to share her hut with a stranger. Christian Garnier is sent to Fiji for what she refers to as a working vacation, until she finds out she has an ornery roommate for the next two weeks who is dead set on making her job twice as hard. Soon, all hell breaks loose and the two women are sent around the world on a wild goose chase.

Stargazing by Kathy L. Salt. Lissa stared open-mouthed at the GIF that played over and over on the screen in front of her. Heat flushed to her face, igniting her skin. Her heart started pounding in her chest. *Stupid internet, it should really come with a warning label.* She's never been interested in relationships or sex and as the years have gone by she has retreated more and more into her work. Everything changes when she meets Star, a porn actress with a heart of gold and a troubled childhood. *They say that opposites attract, but how much of that is true? What chance do they have when one of them is a virgin and the other one star in pornography?*

A New Beginning by KD Rye. There's a quietness, an empty space, that surrounds your life after losing someone you love. Autumn lives in that empty space, day after day, following the same routine, in unresolved angst. She doesn't know how to keep her head above water until the arrival of May, a mysterious dream-like girl who just moved in. Autumn finds refuge in their quickly defined friendship. As her mother falls deeper into depression, Autumn doesn't see a way out of her current situation, until May shows her that anything is possible. However, nothing is what it seems and Autumn has to decipher if the relationship she has built with May is real.

I Belong with Her by Domina Alexandra. Tajel Pierce loves the thrill of being a paramedic. Every call she goes on gives her a rush. She makes no time for a personal life. No one can ruin her love for her career. Then there is Arianna Castaldi, who just transferred to her new paramedic position in a whole new state. All she needs is a new start without any distractions. Arianna and Tajel's relationship doesn't start off perfect. Embarrassed of the one night stand Arianna believes she had with Tajel, she wants to pretend they never met and make their relationship strictly business. The only choice they have to keep from strangling each other is to go from denying their feelings to accepting them as they work through intense 911 calls.

Awakened by Fate by Lynn Lawler. Jackie is a woman living life according to her own rules. She's married, but it's the unspoken, open kind. She can have as many female lovers as she likes; she just can't talk about them. After a bizarre encounter turns her world upside down, things slowly begin to change. She finds herself in desperation as she searches for answers. What she discovers is nothing is delivered in a neatly wrapped box. Now that everything has been brought out into the open, she finds she can't run away from her truth anymore. With her new life, comes new responsibilities and a different outcome than what she was expecting. Jackie isn't alone in the story. She meets several new people who help her along her journey.

Domina Alexandra

Nautical Delights by S. L. Gape. Lady Elizabeth Barrington has spent her entire life trying to please her family; constantly opting for a quiet life, she utilises her profession as a doctor to keep out of her families' clutches; bar the annual two-week Caribbean private cruise, where there is simply no budge. Confined to two weeks on board the Iconica super yacht, she intends on keeping her head down and enjoying as much of the holiday as she can, whilst keeping her family at arm's length. Until a crew member catches her eye.

Whispers of the Heart by KA Moll. Days after completing her fellowship in pediatric ophthalmology, thirty-five-year-old Aki Williams travels from her home in Los Angeles to a small town in Illinois, interviewing for a job that she doesn't want. What she does want is to meet her biological sister, Jack Camdon, a sister whom she didn't know existed until she dreamt of her. Three years ago on Sunday, forty-three-year-old professor of archaeology, Carsyn Lyndon, lost her parents and her wife in a tragic accident. Since then, she's suffered from PTSD and loneliness. She's kind-hearted and handsome but dates no one. When she meets Aki at her four-year-old Godson's birthday party, they're incredibly attracted to one another, and those feelings intensify during a family camping trip—a particularly interesting development for Aki since prior to that she'd never considered that she might be a lesbian.

Worlds Apart by S.L. Gape. Hollywood A-lister Heidi Spencer-Brady is everything you'd expect of an Idol. Loved by all, the British Beauty is graceful, talented, humble and so far removed from the 'typical'

LA scene. When her husband's infidelity with his new 'leading lady' is leaked, Dawn, Heidi's best friend and manager, goes all out to protect her. She arranges for Heidi to go back to the UK and stay on her cousins farm they had visited as children, much to the disappointment of the animal fearing Heidi.

Castor Valley (Law & Order Series Book 2) by Graysen Morgen. Jessie Henry is torn when she reads about the capture of the Doyle brothers, two young men who were part of her old gang. Unable to let them hang for a crime she's sure they didn't commit, Jessie leaves her wife and the Town of Boone Creek behind, and sets out on a journey back to the one place she thought she'd never see again, *Castor Valley*. Ellie Henry watches the love of her life leave, not knowing if she will ever return. When she gets an odd telegram, nearly a week later, she fears Jessie is in trouble. With no other choice, she goes to the one person who can help her.

Close Enough to Touch by Cade Brogan. Joanna Grey injects the deadly poison into the chamber of the syringe—time after time. She's murdered before and she'll do it again. She's intelligent, educated, and beautiful. Rylee Hayes is a respected homicide detective. Her best friends are her grandparents, her coonhound, and her partner—in that order. Kenzie Bigham is the single mom of a thirteen-year-old, a church secretary, and a woman who's struggled much of her adult life with her own sexuality. Their paths will cross when Rylee's new investigation involves members of Kenzie's congregation. Will Rylee have what it takes to meet the challenge of a serial killer who's proven herself to be a more than worthy opponent?

Fight to the Top by S. L. Gape. Georgia is a forty year old, single, Area Director from Manchester, UK who is all work and definitely no play. Having no time to socialise or spend time with her family she prides herself on being fit and well-polished. Erika is an Area Director for the same company, but in the United States. Whilst she is concentrating so heavily on the promotion she has been fighting for, she's starting to feel like her life outside of work is falling apart. The two women are exceptionally different, and worlds apart. Both of their lives are turned upside down when their jobs are snatched from under their noses, and they are suddenly faced with being thrown together by their bosses for one last major project...in Texas.

Boone Creek (Law & Order Series book 1) by Graysen Morgen. Jessie Henry is looking for a new life. She's unknown in the town of Boone Creek when she arrives, and wants to keep it that way. When she's offered the job of Town Marshal, she takes it, believing that protecting others and upholding the law is the penance for her past. Ellie Fray is a widowed, shopkeeper. She generally keeps to herself, but the mysterious new Town Marshal both intrigues and infuriates her. She believes the last thing the town needs is someone stirring up trouble with the outlaws who have taken over.

Witness by Joan L. Anderson. Becca and Kate have lived together for eight years, and have always spent their vacation in a tropical paradise, lying on a beach. This year, Becca wanted to try something different: a seven day, 65-mile hike in the beautiful Cascade Mountains of Washington state. Their peaceful vacation turns to horror when they stumble upon a brutal murder taking place in the back country.

Too Soon by S.L. Gape. Brooke is a twenty-nine year old detective from Oxford, who has her life pretty much planned out until her boss and partner of nine years, Maria, tells her their relationship is over. When Brooke finds out the truth, that Maria cheated on her with their best friend Paula, she decides to get her life back on track by getting away for six weeks in Anglesey, North Wales. Chloe, a thirty three year old artist and art director, owns a log cabin on Anglesey where she spends each weekend painting and surfing. After returning from a surf, she stumbles upon the somewhat uptight and enigmatic Brooke.

Blue Ice Landing by KA Moll. Coy is a beautiful blonde with a southern accent and a successful practice as a physician assistant. She has a comfortable home, good friends, and a loving family. She's also a widow, carrying a burden of responsibility for her wife's untimely death. Coby is a woman with secrets. She's estranged from her family, a recovering alcoholic, and alone because she's convinced that she's unlovable. When she loses her job as a heavy equipment operator, she'll accept one that'll force her to step way outside her comfort zone. When Coy quits her job to accept a position in Antarctica, her path will cross with Coby's. Their attraction to one another will be immediate, and despite their differences, it won't be long before they fall in love. But for these two, with all their baggage, will love be enough?

Never Quit (Never Series book 2) by Graysen Morgen. Two years after stepping away from the action as a Coast Guard Rescue Swimmer to become an instructor, Finley finds herself in charge of the most difficult class of cadets she's ever faced, while also juggling the taxing demands of having a home life with her partner Nicole, and their fifteen year old daughter. Jordy Ross gave up everything, dropping out of college, and leaving her family behind, to join the Coast Guard and become a rescue swimmer cadet. The extreme training tests her fitness level, pushing her mentally and physically further than she's ever been in her life, but it's the aggressive competition between her and another female cadet that proves to be the most challenging.

For a Moment's Indiscretion by KA Moll. With ten years of marriage under their belt, Zane and Jaina are coasting. The little things they used to do for one another have fallen by the wayside. They've gotten busy with life. They've forgotten to nurture their love and relationship. Even soul mates can stumble on hard times and have marital difficulties. Enter Amelia, a new faculty member in Jaina's building. She's new in town, young, and very pretty. When an argument with Zane causes Jaina to storm out angry, she reaches out to Amelia. Of course, she seizes the opportunity. And for a moment of indiscretion, Jaina could lose everything.

Never Let Go (Never Series book 1) by Graysen Morgen. For Coast Guard Rescue Swimmer, Finley

Morris, life is good. She loves her job, is well respected by her peers, and has been given an opportunity to take her career to the next level. The only thing missing is the love of her life, who walked out, taking their daughter with her, seven years earlier. When Finley gets a call from her ex, saying their teenage daughter is coming to spend the summer with her, she's floored. While spending more time with her daughter, whom she doesn't get to see often, and learning to be a full-time parent, Finley quickly realizes she has not, and will never, let go of what is important.

Pursuit by Joan L. Anderson. Claire is a workaholic attorney who flies to Paris to lick her wounds after being dumped by her girlfriend of seventeen years. On the plane she chats with the young woman sitting next to her, and when they land the woman is inexplicably detained in Customs. Claire is surprised when she later runs into the woman in the city. They agree to meet for breakfast the next morning, but when the woman doesn't show up Claire goes to her hotel and makes a horrifying discovery. She soon finds herself ensnared in a web of intrigue and international terrorism, becoming the target of a high stakes game of cat and mouse through the streets of Paris.

Wrecked by Sydney Canyon. To most people, the *Duchess* is a myth formed by old pirates tales, but to Reid Cavanaugh, a Caribbean island bum and one of the best divers and treasure hunters in the world, it's a real, seventeenth century pirate ship—the holy grail of underwater treasure hunting. Reid uses the same cunning tactics she always has before setting out to find the lost ship. However, she is forced to bring her business partner's daughter along as collateral this time because he doesn't trust her. Neither woman is thrilled, but being cooped up on a small dive boat for days, forces them to get know each other quickly.

Arson by Austen Thorne. Madison Drake is a detective for the Stetson Beach Police Department. The last thing she wants to do is show a new detective the ropes, especially when a fire investigation becomes arson to cover up a murder. Madison butts heads with Tara, her trainee, deals with sarcasm from Nic, her ex-girlfriend who is a patrol officer, and finds calm in the chaos of police work with Jamie, her best friend who is the county medical examiner. Arson is the first of many in a series of novella episodes surrounding the fictional Stetson Beach Police Department and Detective Madison Drake.

Change of Heart by KA Moll. Courtney Holloman is a woman at the top of her game. She's successful, wealthy, and a highly sought after Washington lobbyist. She has money, her job, booze, and nothing else. In quiet moments, against her will, her mind drifts back to her days in high school and to all that she gave up. Jack Camdon is a complex woman, and yet not at all. She is also a woman who has never moved beyond the sudden and unexplained departure of her high school sweetheart, her lover, and her soul mate. When circumstances bring Courtney back to town two decades later, their paths will cross. Will it be too late?

Mommies (Bridal Series book 3) **by Graysen Morgen.** Britton and her wife Daphne have been married for a year and a half and are happy with their life, until

Britton's mother hounds her to find out why her sister Bridget hasn't decided to have children yet. This prompts Daphne to bring up the big subject of having kids of their own with Britton. Britton hadn't really thought much about having kids, but her love for Daphne makes her see life and their future together in a whole new way when they decide to become mommies.

***Haunting Love* by K.A. Moll.** Anna Crestwood was raised in the strict beliefs of a religious sect nestled in the foothills of the Smoky Mountains. She's a lesbian with a ton of baggage—fearful, guilty, and alone. Very few things would compel her to leave the familiar. The job offer of a lifetime is one of them. Gabe Garst is a police officer. She's also a powerful medium. Her work with juvenile delinquents and ghosts is all that keeps her going. Inside she's dead, certain that her capacity to love is buried six feet under. Anna and Gabe's paths cross. Their attraction is immediate, but they hold back until all hope seems lost.

***Rapture & Rogue* by Sydney Canyon.** Taren Rauley is happy and in a good relationship, until the one person she thought she'd never see again comes back into her life. She struggles to keep the past from colliding with the present as old feelings she thought were dead and gone, begin to haunt her. In college, Gianna Revisi was a mastermind, ring-leading, crime boss. Now, she has a great life and spends her time running Rapture and Rogue, the two establishments she built from the ground up. The last person she ever expects to see walk into one of them, is the girl who walked out on her, breaking her heart five years ago.

Second Chance by Sydney Canyon. After an attack on her convoy, Marine Corps Staff Sergeant, Darien Hollister, must learn to live without her sight. When an experimental procedure allows her to see again, Darien is torn, knowing someone had to die in order for this to happen.

She embarks on a journey to personally thank the donor's family, but is too stunned to tell them the truth. Mixed emotions stir inside of her as she slowly gets to the know the people that feel like so much more than strangers to her. When the truth finally comes out, Darien walks away, taking the second chance that she's been given to go back to the only life she's ever known, but she's not the only one with a second chance at life.

Meant to Be by Graysen Morgen. Brandt is about to walk down the aisle with her girlfriend, when an unexpected chain of events turns her world upside down, causing her to question the last three years of her life. A chance encounter sparks a mix of rage and excitement that she has never felt before. Summer is living life and following her dreams, all the while, harboring a huge secret that could ruin her career. She believes that some things are better kept in the dark, until she has her third run-in with a woman she had hoped to never see again, and gives into temptation. Brandt and Summer start believing everything happens for a reason as they learn the true meaning of meant to be.

Coming Home by Graysen Morgen. After tragedy derails TJ Abernathy's life, she packs up her three year old son and heads back to Pennsylvania to live with her grandmother on the family farm. TJ picks back up where

A Night Claimed

she left off eight years earlier, tending to the fruit and nut tree orchard, while learning her grandmother's secret trade. Soon, TJ's high school sweetheart and the same girl who broke her heart, comes back into her life, threatening to steal it away once again. As the weeks turn into months and tragedy strikes again, TJ realizes coming home was the best thing she could've ever done.

Special Assignment by Austen Thorne. Secret Service Agent Parker Meeks has her hands full when she gets her new assignment, protecting a Congressman's teenage daughter, who has had threats made on her life and been whisked away to a Christian boarding school under an alias to finish out her senior year. Parker is fine with the assignment, until she finds out she has to go undercover as a Canon Priest. The last thing Parker expects to find is a beautiful, art history teacher, who is intrigued by her in more ways than one.

Miracle at Christmas by Sydney Canyon. A Modern Twist on the Classic Scrooge Story. Dylan is a power-hungry lawyer who pushed away everything good in her life to become the best defense attorney in the, often winning the worst cases and keeping anyone with enough money out of jail. She's visited on Christmas Eve by her deceased law partner, who threatens her with a life in hell like his own, if she doesn't change her path. During the course of the night, she is taken on a journey through her past, present, and future with three very different spirits.

Bella Vita by Sydney Canyon. Brady is the First Officer of the crew on the Bella Vita, a luxury charter yacht in the Caribbean. She enjoys the laidback island lifestyle, and is accustomed to high profile guests, but when a U.S. Senator charters the yacht as a gift to his beautiful twin daughters who have just graduated from college and a few of their friends, she literally has her hands full.

Brides (Bridal Series book 2) by Graysen Morgen. Britton Prescott is dating the love of her life, Daphne Attwood, after a few tumultuous events that happened to unravel at her sister's wedding reception, seven months earlier. She's happy with the way things are, but immense pressure from her family and friends to take the next step, nearly sends her back to the single life. The idea of a long engagement and simple wedding are thrown out the window, as both families take over, rushing Britton and Daphne to the altar in a matter of weeks.

Cypress Lake by Graysen Morgen. The small town of Cypress Lake is rocked when one murder after another happens. Dani Ricketts, the Chief Deputy for the Cypress Lake Sheriff's Office, realizes the murders are linked. She's surprised when the girl that broke her heart in high school has not only returned home, but she's also Dani's only suspect. Kristen Malone has come back to Cypress Lake to put the past behind her so that she can move on with her life. Seeing Dani Ricketts again throws her off-guard, nearly derailing her plans to finally rid herself and her family of Cypress Lake.

Crashing Waves by Graysen Morgen. After a tragic accident, Pro Surfer, Rory Eden, spends her days hiding in the surf and snowboard manufacturing company that she built from the ground up, while living her life as a shell of the person that she once was. Rory's world is turned upside when a young surfer pursues her, asking for the one thing she can't do. Adler Troy and Dr. Cason Macauley from Graysen Morgen's bestselling novel: *Falling Snow*, make an appearance in this romantic adventure about life, love, and letting go.

Bridesmaid of Honor (Bridal Series book 1) by Graysen Morgen. Britton Prescott's best friend is getting married and she's the maid of honor. As if that isn't enough to deal with, Britton's sister announces she's getting married in the same month and her maid of honor is her best friend Daphne, the same woman who has tormented Britton for years. Britton has to suck it up and play nice, instead of scratching her eyes out, because she and Daphne are in both weddings. Everyone is counting on them to behave like adults.

Falling Snow by Graysen Morgen. Dr. Cason Macauley, a high-speed trauma surgeon from Denver meets Adler Troy, a professional snowboarder and sparks fly. The last thing Cason wants is a relationship and Adler doesn't realize what's right in front of her until it's gone, but will it be too late?

Fate vs. Destiny by Graysen Morgen. Logan Greer devotes her life to investigating plane crashes for the National Transportation Safety Board. Brooke McCabe is an investigator with the Federal Aviation Association who literally flies by the seat of her pants. When Logan gets tangled in head games with both women will she choose fate or destiny?

Just Me by Graysen Morgen. Wild child Ian Wiley has to grow up and take the reins of the hundred year old family business when tragedy strikes. Cassidy Harland is a little surprised that she came within an inch of picking up a gorgeous stranger in a bar and is shocked to find out that stranger is the new head of her company.

Love Loss Revenge by Graysen Morgen. Rian Casey is an FBI Agent working the biggest case of her career and madly in love with her girlfriend. Her world is turned upside when tragedy strikes. Heartbroken, she tries to rebuild her life. When she discovers the truth behind what really happened that awful night she decides justice isn't good enough, and vows revenge on everyone involved.

Natural Instinct by Graysen Morgen. Chandler Scott is a Marine Biologist who keeps her private life private. Corey Joslen is intrigued by Chandler from the moment she meets her. Chandler is forced to finally open her life up to Corey. It backfires in Corey's face and sends her running. Will either woman learn to trust her natural instinct?

Secluded Heart by Graysen Morgen. Chase Leery is an overworked cardiac surgeon with a group of best friends that have an opinion and a reason for everything. When she meets a new artist named Remy Sheridan at her best friend's art gallery she is captivated by the reclusive woman. When Chase finds out why Remy is so sheltered will she put her career on the line to help her or is it too difficult to love someone with a secluded heart?

A Night Claimed

In Love, at War by Graysen Morgen. Charley Hayes is in the Army Air Force and stationed at Ford Island in Pearl Harbor. She is the commanding officer of her own female-only service squadron and doing the one thing she loves most, repairing airplanes. Life is good for Charley, until the day she finds herself falling in love while fighting for her life as her country is thrown haphazardly into World War II. Can she survive being in love and at war?

Fast Pitch by Graysen Morgen. Graham Cahill is a senior in college and the catcher and captain of the softball team. Despite being an all-star pitcher, Bailey Michaels is young and arrogant. Graham and Bailey are forced to get to know each other off the field in order to learn to work together on the field. Will the extra time pay off or will it drive a nail through the team?

Submerged by Graysen Morgen. Assistant District Attorney Layne Carmichael had no idea that the sexy woman she took home from a local bar for a one night stand would turn out to be someone she would be prosecuting months later. Scooter is a Naval Officer on a submarine who changes women like she changes uniforms. When she is accused of a heinous crime she is shocked to see her latest conquest sitting across from her as the prosecuting attorney.

Vow of Solitude by Austen Thorne. Detective Jordan Denali is in a fight for her life against the ghosts from her past and a Serial Killer taunting her with his every move. She lives a life of solitude and plans to keep it that way. When Callie Marceau, a curious Medical Examiner, decides she wants in on the biggest case of her career, as well as, Jordan's life, Jordan is powerless to stop her.

Igniting Temptation by Sydney Canyon. Mackenzie Trotter is the Head of Pediatrics at the local hospital. Her life takes a rather unexpected turn when she meets a flirtatious, beautiful fire fighter. Both women soon discover it doesn't take much to ignite temptation.

One Night by Sydney Canyon. While on a business trip, Caylen Jarrett spends an amazing night with a beautiful stripper. Months later, she is shocked and confused when that same woman re-enters her life. The fact that this stranger could destroy her career doesn't bother her. C.J. is more terrified of the feelings this woman stirs in her. Could she have fallen in love in one night and not even known it?

Fine by Sydney Canyon. Collin Anderson hides behind a façade, pretending everything is fine. Her workaholic wife and best friend are both oblivious as she goes on an emotional journey, battling a potentially hereditary disease that her mother has been diagnosed with. The only person who knows what is really going on, is Collin's doctor. The same doctor, who is an acquaintance that she's always been attracted to, and who has a partner of her own.

Shadow's Eyes by Sydney Canyon. Tyler McCain is the owner of a large ranch that breeds and sells different types of horses. She isn't exactly thrilled when a Hollywood movie producer shows up wanting to film his latest movie on her property. Reegan Delsol is an up and coming actress who has everything going for her when she lands the lead role in a new film, but there one small problem that could blow the entire picture.

Light Reading: A Collection of Novellas by Sydney Canyon. Four of Sydney Canyon's novellas together in one book, including the bestsellers Shadow's Eyes and One Night.

Visit us at www.tri-pub.com